Imperious

The Shadow Illuminist

Nitin Sharma

Ukiyoto Publishing

All global publishing rights are held by

Ukiyoto Publishing

Published in 2023

Content Copyright © Nitin Sharma

ISBN 9789360493257

All rights reserved.

No part of this publication may be reproduced, transmitted, or stored in a retrieval system, in any form by any means, electronic, mechanical, photocopying, recording or otherwise, without the prior permission of the publisher.

The moral rights of the author have been asserted.

This is a work of fiction. Names, characters, businesses, places, events, locales, and incidents are either the products of the author's imagination or used in a fictitious manner. Any resemblance to actual persons, living or dead, or actual events is purely coincidental.

This book is sold subject to the condition that it shall not by way of trade or otherwise, be lent, resold, hired out or otherwise circulated, without the publisher's prior consent, in any form of binding or cover other than that in which it is published.

www.ukiyoto.com

Contents

The Old Beginning	1
The First Chase	10
The Second Chase	21
Where One's Wit's End	31
The Third And The Fourth Chase	37
The Super Cop	48
The Decision	56
Finding The One	63
The Fifth Chase	73
The Apprence Of Devil	84
The Reveal Of Truth	89
The Good Vs The Bad	96
The Ultimate Clue	105
The Final Chase	116
About the Author	*126*

The Old Beginning

In 1914, West Bengal

There was a small village nearby in Malda district. Where the majority of the dwellings were made of mud, just a few houses were made of baked bricks. An aunt and her 8-year-old nephew used to live in such a mud house.

One evening, the child returned to his home after playing and found that his aunt was griding some leaves on the griding stone. He came and sat next to her.

"Why do you make me drink this leaf juice daily?" the boy asked.

Aunt grinned.

"With this, no one will know your secret, and you will become stronger," she said.

"Ohh! You know, Sagar's grandpa told us a story of the devil, but he said that devils are dangerous and wicked," the boy said.

"No, my boy." She stopped grinding and looked at him.

"Well, tell me, how many elements are humans made of?"

"Five!" the boy replied. "Air, fire, water, sky, and soil"

"Very nice, but the devils are made of only 3 elements. Fire, water, and the most important blood Now, tell me who is easy to kill," the aunt asked.

"Devil" the boy replied in a second.

"But then why is everybody afraid of them?"

"Because the devil always conceals his true body. People were unable to find it and then began to fear them as a result," the aunt said.

The boy's curiosity grew even more, but his aunt put a stop to it by giving him the juice to drink.

In 2022, Goa.

In the western section of Goa, there is a town named Old Goa, which is situated at the Mandovi river. It was famous for its ancient churches, Indian-Portuguese mixed culture, and breath-taking scenery, but for a century it was notorious for "The Perigoso".

Perigoso was the name of the central forest located in the centre of old Goa. It links the town to the main market. The main market is approximately 800 metres from the Perigoso. The Perigoso is shaped like a pentagon and has five entrances, the first of which is in the north and connects to the main market. The remaining four were in the north-east, the south-east, the south-west, and the north-west.

Because the people of this town were terrified of the forest, they gave it the name Perigoso, which means "dangerous." They were afraid that some terrible power had taken control of the forest, so they posted a warning sign there as well. Every year, a corpse is found in the forest.

One day on a dazzling morning, a biker stopped his bike near a huge signboard that said 'Welcome to Old Goa.' He was 5'9" tall and in his mid-twenties. He took off his helmet. His skin was fair; he had short hair, was clean-shaven, had brown eyes, and had a lean body, but his sharp triceps peered through his white t-shirt. He donned a green jogger and a pair of white sneakers. He looked at the board and smiled, then he wore his helmet and entered old Goa. He saw markets, parks, churches, and the Perigoso while riding.

He came a halt in front of a house. Every house in that neighbourhood had a tiny garden. He got off his bike and proceeded to the door, where he rang the doorbell.

"Coming!" a feminine voice came from inside.

Within 10 seconds, the door opened, and a girl emerged. Her age was 37, but she kept herself in such good shape that she appeared to be in her early thirties. She was dressed in a blue peplum top with white regular jean.

"Sakshi," the biker said.

Sakshi was ecstatic to see the rider.

"Poonish, bhaiya," she said and embraced him.

"Shh! Somebody will listen," Poonish said.

"Come". Poonish entered, and Sakshi led him to the drawing room. On one side of the room, there was a couch and a beanbag next to it. In front of the couch, a table with a stack of magazines was kept. On the left side of the couch was a bookshelf, and on the right side was a large window that let light into the room. Several photo frames were hung on the front wall of the couch.

"You relax; I'll make you coffee," Sakshi stated as she headed to the kitchen. Poonish sat on the couch, taking in his surroundings. Meanwhile, Sakshi brought him coffee and gave him the coffee mug. She sat next to him on the couch as well.

"It's been really so long since we met," she started remembering. "I think at Grandpa's funeral?"

"Yes," Poonish said, taking a sip of coffee and then saying, "After that, I just keep running and running for my life."

"You are blessed," she said.

"It's not a blessing, it's a curse" he said.

"How long will you run like this? Why don't you stay here with me? Together, we can handle it." She spoke.

Poonish stood up and walked over to the window, where he looked out.

"The moment we are born, we are pursued by sorrow. We can't win from it, but we can hide from it by having as few relations as possible, which is what I'm doing."

"But when we are with the family, we can easily handle any kind of situation," she said.

Silence took over the room. Poonish turned back to Sakshi.

"I'm here for a week, so can we just live the moments as we did in our childhood?" he asked.

"You mean as in my childhood?" she guffawed.

Poonish smiled and nodded his head.

Then Poonish put the coffee mug on the table and said in an exciting way, "Three of us will enjoy this week as much as," suddenly Sakshi interrupted him and spoke.

"Three of us, who is the third one?"

"Chinki!" he replied.

"Chinki? Your girlfriend?" Sakshi asked in a teasing way.

"My bike," he emphasised.

"Chinki, seriously," she laughed out loud.

Poonish gave her a strange look.

"Okay! Okay! You can relax with your Chinki," she emphasised on Chinki. I have to go to the office."

"What about our excursion?" Poonish was startled, said

"It starts tomorrow; if you are hungry, there are some apples in the fridge. Bye," Sakshi said.

Poonish took a deep breath and said, "okay! Bye"

They began their weekly vacation the following morning. They travelled to various locations, ate some new and unique meals, visited beaches, went surfing, visited churches and monuments, took several photographs, and had a great time.

At the weekend, Poonish was packing his belongings into the room, with the door partially open. Sakshi came there and paused at the threshold. She seemed mournful. She then entered the room and sat on a bed corner.

"Have you finished packing?" She asked.

"Yup, almost," he replied.

"Where do you go next?" She asked another question.

"I have no idea, where the winds will take me." Poonish replied with a smile, but Sakshi looked gloomy.

Poonish took a step and sat beside her. "What happen?"

"Loneliness is the hardest thing that you have to suffer. It's like you have everything except yourself," she said.

"You know who I am; it's hard to stay, but I'll promise, I'll be with you on your every birthday. Now, smile, please... please... for me."

Sakshi's lips were lightly touched by a smile.

He went for a walk in the evening after packing things. He was passing through the Perigoso, suddenly, he came to a halt and stared at it. A longing arose in him to see the forest. Although Sakshi had repeatedly prevented him from going inside, but it's human nature to do the work for which he is forbidden. Poonish adopted this nature as well and entered the forest.

"Among all the things, nature is always beautiful." He exclaimed.

He was enchanted by the forest. As he continued on, he noticed more lovely foliage.

A strange butterfly with black wings and a red body appeared out of nowhere. Poonish lost himself and stared at it.

"Gorgeous,"

The weather suddenly changed, and fog blanketed the forest.

"The weather didn't change as quickly in coastal areas, but this is unusual." He spoke.

He felt someone behind him in the fog, so he turned around, but there was no one.

He had a feeling something was not right, so he decided to return, but he couldn't see his way out due to the fog. He felt someone behind him again, so he turned around, but no one was there again.

"Hello, is someone here?" He shouted.

A shadow with big red eyes darted towards Poonish and crossed across his body, emerging from the dark fog. As a result, he fainted and fell to the ground.

When he recovered consciousness, he found himself at the entrance of the forest. He looked around, wondering how he got here. His head was aching, so he stood up, holding his head.

"Why can't I remember anything?" he said.

The evening was turning into the night, and the streetlights were on, so he decided to go home and forget about this incident. He walked away from there, but his shadow was still lying on the ground. The shadow dissipated on its own after a minute.

His shadow was not with him when he returned home.

Sakshi was working in the kitchen. When she saw Poonish, she asked, "What happened?" You looked tired."

"Nothing" he replied.

"Go wash your hands quickly; I've made dinner and also some cookies for tomorrow," she added, leaving food on the dining table.

"Sakshi!" he said.

"yes", she replied.

"I'm not going anywhere", he exclaimed.

Sakshi was surprised to hear this and said, "Are you alright?"

"I've realised the value of a family now. You are the last member of my family, and I can't lose you," he said emotionally.

"I'm pleased with your decision," Sakshi responded with a smile.

Both were happy and enjoying their meal.

The First Chase

From the next morning on, life flows as it flows. Poonish used to stay at home and get bored, while Sakshi used to go to her office. One day, he had the idea to look for a job. He didn't typically consider himself to be a '9 to 5' type of person, but when he started his new life, he realised he needed a job too, so he began looking for jobs in the newspaper.

He liked a job as an accountant that was listed in a gallery after perusing numerous advertisements, and because he qualified for it, he grabbed his phone and scheduled an interview for the following morning.

The next morning, he hurriedly got ready. When Sakshi inquired, he replied that he was going for an interview. Sakshi wished him the best of luck. He started his bike and left the house, but his bike broke down in the middle of the road.

"No! no! no! "Not this time," he said tingly.

He attempted to start the bike but failed. He became frustrated and sat on the pavement.

A girl was driving by in a jeep. She had a lovely, radiant face and a slim physique. She was 5'7" tall and roughly 23 years old, and her hair was tied in a ponytail. She was dressed in a baby pink crop top, a white open shirt with jeans shorts, light green slip-on sneakers on her feet, a bracelet in her right hand, and a locket with the letter P around her neck.

She noticed a boy sitting on the pavement next to a bike. She came to a halt and asked, "Are you okay?"

Poonish eyes were fixated on her. She was quite enchanting.

"I have an interview, and my bike refuses to take me there."

The girl guffawed.

"Where are you going for the interview?" she inquired.

Poonish provided her with the address.

"If you are running late, I'll drop you off."

"Thank you so much but my bike?" Poonish was perplexed.

"Relax, it's Goa; nobody is going to steal your bike," she said.

Poonish had a thought at that precise moment. He took his bike up to the flower stall in front of him. He requested the person at the stall to look over his bike and said he'd be back in an hour. He also bought a bouquet of Lilly and returned to that girl, sat in the jeep, and they drove away.

"Want to make an impression on the interviewer," the girl said as she glanced at the flowers.

"NO!", he remarked.

"Now, the staller will actually have an eye on my bike," he said.

"You're smart enough," she said.

"A little bit," he said, and they both guffawed.

They were at his destination in barely 15 minutes.

"Break a leg," the girl wished him.

Poonish grabbed the flowers, extended them to that girl, and thanked her.

The girl glanced at the flowers for a second and thought something, but then she smiled and accepted the flowers.

"Pleasure, see you," she said as she left away.

Poonish gazed at the building, which had a name board with the words "Music with the Notes" printed in big letters on it. He was thinking that it wasn't a gallery but rather a three-floor book and musical instrument store. He then entered.

There were many people in the gallery, some of whom were wearing a blue half-sleeve t-shirt with the gallery's name inscribed on it. Poonish inquired as to the whereabouts of Mr. Arman Solanki. He was told that Arman would be in his cabin on the second floor.

He followed the directions and arrived at the cabin.

Arman sat in a chair. There was a table in front of him and two chairs in front of the table. A fourth of the room was occupied by some empty boxes.

Arman's age was almost the same as that of Poonish. He was born in Delhi but had spent the last few years running his gallery in Goa.

"May I come in?" Poonish knocked on the door.

"Yes! Please come in." Arman invited him in.

"I've come for an interview," Poonish said.

"Poonish Dasgupta?" Arman confirmed.

Poonish gave a nod.

Arman motioned for him to take a seat. Poonish sat down and handed him his resume.

Arman was poring over the resume.

"As I'm seeing, you did your schooling in M.P., your graduation from Delhi, and your P.G. from Bengaluru, why?" Arman asked.

"Because of my grandpa's transfers, he was in the Air Force." Poonish said.

"Grandpa"?

"I haven't seen my parents." Poonish said.

"Oh! Sorry"

"You did your P.G. in 2015 but are still a greenhorn?" Arman asked.

"I was a traveller; that's why," Poonish said.

"You have been travelling for the last 5 years; how did you suddenly consider a job?"

"I believe now is the time to be serious in life," Poonish replied.

"If I have experience one and you, why would I choose you?" Arman asked.

"He may have experience in this particular job, but I have life experience, so I can assist you with other things as well," Poonish responded.

"Impressive, I also want a multiplayer. Congratulations! You've got the job," Arman said, and then they shook hands.

Poonish felt that it was easy to give an interview.

"I'd like to ask you a question," Poonish said.

Arman simply smiled and said, "I know what you're going to ask; look, this is Goa; people come here to enjoy; they want a break from their boring lives, not to do the same stuff as they do."

Arman stood and said "Come, I'll introduce you to everyone"

They proceeded to the first floor, where Arman escorted him to a room. He stated that it was for our VIP clients. The first floor had two desks in the corner. He remarked to Poonish, "The vacant one is yours," while a girl was sitting on the other.

Her hairstyle was bob cut, and a strip of her hair was burgundy-tinted. She was 28 years old. She was dressed in t-shirt and sweatpants.

"Meet Garima; she handles our online stuff, and he's Poonish, our new accountant," Arman introduced them.

Garima was a bit busy, so she just said hello to Poonish and started doing her work again.

Then they proceeded to the ground floor. Arman introduced Poonish to a boy with curly hair. The boy was preparing a list of goods.

"He is Atul, our inventory manager, and Poonish, our accountant."

They exchanged handshakes. "Welcome to the family, buddy," Atul said.

A customer called before Atul finished his sentence. Just then, another guy with massive biceps who looked like a bodybuilder arrived to show Arman a letter. Poonish and the boy named Sahil had introduced themselves, by the time Arman was glancing at the letter. Then Arman discussed something with Sahil.

Meanwhile, the same girl who helped Poonish came there and congratulated him. Poonish was surprised to see her because she was likewise wearing a blue t-shirt.

"Do I know you?" Poonish said it amusingly.

"I give people rides in exchange for flowers," the girl said.

They laughed.

"She's Priyanka, our supervisor and cashier," Arman said after talking with Sahil about the letter.

"Although we are all family, but Priyanka and Garima are true sisters."

"However, I'm more sensible." Priyanka said, and all of them laughed.

Atul summoned Priyanka from behind the counter to prepare a bill. So, she went there, and Sahil took care of the customers.

"This is my family, which I earned here; we are one for all and all for one." Arman said to Poonish.

"I respect your feelings". Poonish stated.

Then they returned to the cabin to complete some paperwork.

Poonish wasn't sure he'd be able to do the work, but he did it so well that he didn't realise a month had passed. He was truly happy this time. Sometimes he raced bikes with Garima, sometimes he played video games with Atul, sometimes he did push-ups with Sahil, which Sahil always won, and Sakshi taught him to cook grandma's special dish, but whenever he met Priyanka, he forgot about himself and got engrossed in her. Priyanka would also listen to his adventure stories. Their attraction to each other grew stronger. In the midst of it all, he forgot that he was abnormal.

An evening, Sakshi and Poonish were in the kitchen. They were preparing dinner. Poonish sat at the dining table, chopping veggies for the salad, while

Sakshi prepared the dessert. The dining table was directly in front of the kitchen. They were having a casual discussion about their jobs.

Suddenly, Poonish looked at Sakshi's shadow, which was approaching in front of him. Poonish quivered and lowered his head when he saw the shadow. He began to murmur something. Sakshi also began humming while cooking. Poonish took a tomato and squeezed it on the shadow, causing all of the juice to fall on the shadow.

Sakshi felt something streaming out of her eyes as the juice dropped down towards the shadow's head, so she cleaned her eyes with a tissue. When she saw blood on the tissue, she panicked and looked at the shelf glass. The blood was flowing from her eyes.

She screamed out to Poonish, but Poonish continued to whisper. So, she tried to approach him but couldn't move her leg. Slowly, slowly, blood poured from her ears and nostrils as well. She screamed and sobbed uncontrollably.

Sakshi's skin cracked, and blood oozed from her skin as the juice poured towards the appendicular. She continued to scream and wail, but no one listened. She fell and died after a while of suffering in this torment. There was a lot of blood on the floor.

After all this, Poonish raised his head, his irisless, blood shot eyes as crimson as hell; he was sweating profusely, and he smiled wickedly at the dead body.

18 Imperious

The next morning, Poonish woke up from his bed. He had normal eyes. He took his customary shower and had no recollection of the previous night. He entered the kitchen, where everything was neatly arranged, and the tomato was placed on the table. There was no sign of blood; it looked immaculate.

He pulled out milk, eggs, and bread from the fridge and asked loudly, "Sakshi, what do you want for breakfast?" He received no response. He repeated it loudly but received no response again. So, he looked in the bathroom for her but couldn't find her. He assumed she had left for the office. He immediately ate his first meal and left the house.

As he passed through the Perigoso, he noticed a considerable gathering at the northern entrance. He came to a halt and went to investigate what had occurred. He noticed a corpse ahead of him, and it was Sakshi's. The body had turned pallid, and there were cracks all over it.

"Sakshi" Poonish shrieked and dashed towards the body, taking Sakshi's head on his lap and wailing.

Arman was also on the same path when he heard the ruckus and approached the gathering. He was flabbergasted by the scene and went straight to Poonish to console him. He felt sorry for Poonish's situation.

After a while, a police inspector whose wrinkles showed his experience and the name Shahzad Khan on his badge appeared, along with a constable who was likewise 45 years old and named Johnny Costa, came to the spot. They separated Poonish from the corpse and started inspecting the body. The inspector intuited it was a horrific murder when he observed the blood marks all over the corpse and the cracked skin. When he spotted Poonish sobbing, he approached him and inquired.

"Which relationship did you have with the dead body?" The inspector asked

Poonish wiped his tears and replied, "He was my sister, Sakshi."

"In my opinion, it is a clear murder; someone who despises Sakshi did it, but we must wait for the forensic report," the inspector stated.

"Do you suspect anyone?"

"No! But if I find him, he'll suffer like this 10 times over," Poonish snarled.

"I know how you feel," the inspector asked Poonish's name?

Poonish told his name.

"You should also be cautious, and if you find something odd, just call me." The inspector said so, and they took the body with them.

Arman and Poonish returned home as well.

Arman summoned everyone to Poonish's home. There were six people in the house, yet the house longed to hear a single word from morning to dusk. Poonish told them not to worry about him when night fell, he stating that he was okay! And sent everyone home. While Priyanka was leaving, she sliced some fruits and told him to call her if he needed anything.

After everyone left, Poonish went to Sakshi's bedroom and laid down on the bed, but as soon as he closed his eyes, Sakshi's memories began to play in front of his eyes like a movie. This time, it was his heart that was crying, not his eyes. "This is the pain; this is the sorrow; I told you," Poonish said.

The Second Chase

The very next morning, grief spread along with the sun's rays. Everyone in the gallery was working as usual, but they were engrossed in Poonish's concerns. Everyone agreed to meet at Poonish's place in the afternoon. Meanwhile, the door of the gallery opened, and Poonish entered. His face was withered, and he had dark circles under his eyes. He didn't appear to have slept since the previous night. Everyone was stunned when they saw him.

"Why have you come? I told you to take leave," Arman said.

"I'm fine," Poonish responded, but his face said otherwise.

He headed towards the 1st floor.

Priyanka stopped him on the way up the stairs and stated, "You are not okay!"

Poonish deliberately ignored her and went towards his desk. Priyanka was astonished by his unusual behaviour.

"Leave him alone for a little while," Arman advised Priyanka.

He sat down and concerted on his PC.

Garima tried to focus on her work, but her gaze was drawn to Poonish's distressed face.

People were immersed in their work as the day progressed. Everyone was prepared to leave as the clock hit six o'clock, except Arman and Sahil, who were working overtime that night.

Garima noticed Poonish walking alone outside. After a thought, she told Priyanka that she had some work, and on this pretext, she sent both Priyanka and Atul.

Two roads used to emerge from the gallery, one on the right and the other on the left. Although Priyanka and Garima's house was on the left, they always dropped Atul off at his house, which was on the right. As a result, Garima sent them home and hurriedly moved to the left road.

"Where is Chinki?" she asked

Poonish came to a halt and looked at Garima, asking, "What are you doing here?"

"I asked first," she said

"In the garage," he responded.

"Why?" she asked.

"I don't feel well," he said, then asked, "And you?"

"To be honest, when I saw you, you looked miserable, and I can't see you like this. I care about you." She stated.

They began to walk.

"It's not the first time someone I love has gone far away from me, but I don't understand why this keeps happening to me," he lamented.

"I understand; my parents died in an accident four years ago, and I was thinking the same thing as you. I couldn't feel anything either, but I had to keep my control for Priyanka. We've got to live for those who care about us," she said.

"Sakshi was the reason I stayed, and now I don't know what to do," he said.

"You have thousands of reasons to leave, but find a reason to stay," she said.

They came to a crossroad in the road where both of their houses were in opposite directions.

"Go home; Priyanka will be waiting," he said.

Garima gave a nod.

"I hope I'll see you tomorrow, bye!" Garima said as she walked away. Poonish also returned home.

The next morning at the gallery, Garima was constantly staring at the stairs. She expected Poonish to come. Her wish was granted, and Poonish entered the gallery. When Priyanka saw him, she greeted him with good morning, but Poonish again ignored her and went to his desk. Garima's face lit up when she saw Poonish. She went to him.

"How do you feel now?" she asked.

Poonish closed his eyes and took a deep breath.

"Amor no ar (love in the air)," he mumbled.

"What"? Sakshi asked.

Poonish glanced at her, smiled, and said "much better", but it was the same smile he had when he saw Sakshi's corpse.

"I'm happy to see you smiling," she said with a smile.

"Me too, and credit goes to you, miss," he said.

"Any information from the inspector?" she inquired.

"Not yet," he replied.

Arman summoned Garima into his cabin, interrupting their conversation.

At the end of the day, Garima did what she did yesterday. She fabricated a pretext and walked with Poonish to the same crossroad, where they said goodnight to each other, and when Garima was leaving, Poonish embraced her. Poonish's gesture made her feel a little awkward, but her heart was filled with affection. She blushed and walked away without saying anything, but Poonish was smiling, and his eyes were crimson.

From that day on, Garima and Poonish started meeting after work. Because of this, they had a lot of attraction for each other. It had been almost a month since they met like this.

On an evening at the crossroads, Poonish grabbed Garima's hand and said, "I'd like you to join me for dinner at my house tomorrow. It's a pleasant request. There's also a surprise for you." He said it in a deep tone.

Garima was conjuring up the idea that Poonish would propose to her.

"Our lives will be changed starting tomorrow", he concluded.

"I'm really looking forward to tomorrow," she remarked with a wide smile.

"Eu tambem (me too)," he whispered and embraced her.

Garima was getting ready for her dinner date on Sunday evening. She donned a red bodycon dress, in which she looked sizzling. Because of the lipstick, her lips were more beautiful and red. A garland of white pearls was also worn around the neck. She had never worn such a dress before, but today was the happiest day of her life. She took the key to the Jeep, but then she realised "Jeep with this dress, bad idea", so she put the key back and booked a cab. Priyanka appeared in front of her as she was about to leave.

"Ohh! Someone is looking like a girl; what's the matter?" Priyanka teased her.

"Nothing," Garima was trying to conceal, but her smile was saying everything.

"There….is……. something,"

"I'm getting late, so I'm going," Garima said.

Priyanka took a position in front of the door.

"First, name, then I'll let you go," Priyanka said.

"Whose name?" Garima was still beaming.

"Don't try to act smart," Priyanka said.

Garima believed that Priyanka would not let her go unless she told her name, so she said, "Okay, I'll tell you, but when I return, now please step aside and let me go."

Priyanka relented, "Have fun," she winked.

Inspector Shazaad and constable Johnny arrived at the forensic science laboratory to meet Doctor Chauhan, who was in charge of the lab as well as this case.

"Do you have any leads?" the inspector inquired.

"Nothing," the doctor replied.

"Not again; you must have something," the inspector said.

"I have examined the body three times. Her body turned pale since she only had half a litre of blood left. I discovered no serious injuries, cuts, or wounds either inside or outside the body. I don't know how these cracks formed, and there's a 0.1% chance they bled directly," the doctor explained.

The inspector appeared tensed.

"Where did you get this corpse?" the doctor asked.

"From the Perigoso," the constable replied.

The doctor startled.

"Shahzad! I'm sick of telling you the same thing," the doctor said.

"I'm also tired of telling you that there is a human behind all this," the inspector said.

The doctor took Shahzad by the hand and took him to a room filled with files. In a corner, there was a stack of Perigoso files.

"If any human has done all this, how come your police department hasn't solved a single case in 111 years?" the doctor said tingly.

"Because you're like my brother, I'm telling you not to waste your time. The rest is up to you," the doctor remarked as he walked away.

Garima, On the other hand, arrived at Poonish's home. Poonish was astonished when he saw her. He was dressed in a combination of a black shirt and blue jeans.

"You are looking drop-dead gorgeous," he said.

"Credit goes to you, Mr." she smiled.

"If I knew you were so hot, I would have dated you a long time ago," he said as he beckoned her inside.

Where there was once a dining table, there are now two chairs and a small round table. A red candle was set in the centre of the table, and two glasses with a bottle of champagne were also placed. The dim lights created a romantic atmosphere. Slow music was playing, making the atmosphere livelier.

"I'm impressed by your surprise," she said as she kissed him on the cheek, leaving a lipstick stain on his cheek.

"It looks like I got your face dirty," she smiled.

"No! Rather, it'll bring me good fortune," he said, gazing her in the eyes.

Then, they approached the table.

Poonish drew the chair for her; she sat on it, and Poonish sat on the other. He uncorked the champagne bottle and poured it into the glasses. One was for Garima, the other for himself.

"For us," she said

"Yes! us," he said.

They cheers and took their first sip.

"I have a reason to stay now. "I've found my way," he said.

"Together, we'll get through all your tough times and create some beautiful memories," Garima stated, interlacing her fingers with Poonish's.

"That's why I chose you." He stood up, approached Garima, and asked her to dance with him. Garima accepted his request and extended her hand.

They began to dance. Poonish had his hands on Garima's waist, and Garima had her hands around Poonish's neck.

"You look more beautiful from closely," he complimented.

"Enough compliments for today," she blushed.

"My life depends on yours, EU te amo senhorita."

"What?"

"I love you, miss" he said.

Her heart was touched with a weird joy, and she smiled.

"I love you too, Mr.," she said, and she was going to kiss him.

As soon as Garima's lips touched Poonish's lips, suddenly Poonish got a shock, and his eyes turned red.

When Garima saw Poonish's red eyes, she exclaimed, "What the hell?"

Poonish promptly picked up Garima's glass of champagne and dipped his three fingers into it.

"Fantoche," he said in a deep tone, and he sprinkled it on Garima's shadow with all three fingers.

Garima's shadow vanished in an instant, and she stood there like a puppet without blinking her eyes.

"I had a fantastic time with you. You're bold and courageous like me, but sorry, I'm in a bit of a hurry, so we'll have to finish this date here," he said as he stood in front of her.

"Repeat after me, my love," he began reciting the spell.

"Eu invoco a morte (I summon the death)

Do subterraneo mais escuro (from the darkest underground)

Para aumentar seu poder e (to enlarge his power and)

Para trocar seu corpo com sombra (to exchange her body with shadow)".

Garima was repeating, her eyes welling up with tears.

He handed Garima a glass of champagne before picking his own.

"Have a safe journey," he smirked as he handed her the glass and ordered her to drink.

Her veins began to turn black as soon as she began drinking. When she finished her drink, all of her veins went dark black, and she fell to the ground and died.

"Outro," he said and laughed

Where One's Wit's End

It was Monday morning, the first day of the week, and everyone was raring to get to work. Poonish had also left his house. He had no recollection of the previous night or Garima. At his house, everything was in its place.

He spotted a crowd again when he passed through the Perigoso, but this time it was at the north-western entrance. When his gaze fell on his pals, he hurriedly approached them and discovered Garima's corpse, which had black lines on her veins and bruises all over it. Priyanka was crying bitterly.

Inspector Shahzad and Constable Johnny are also present. They were shocked to see the corpse.

"How can there be another corpse?" Johnny said to the inspector,

The inspector had worried creases on his brow.

"Search the body and see if you can find anything," the inspector ordered Johnny, keeping himself calm as he came to Priyanka.

"I know it's hard, but we have to do our duty."
"Where was she last night?" the inspector inquired.

"She went out to dinner with a friend." Priyanka sobbed.

"Which friend?"

"I don't know," she said.

"Do you have any ideas where they could go?" the inspector asked.

Priyanka nodded in no.

"Have you noticed anything odd?" the inspector asked. But Priyanka's answer was again "no."

"Think of anything that can help us,"

"She loved her Jeep more than herself, but last night she booked a cab," Priyanka said after thinking.

"Which company was it?" the inspector asked.

"I didn't notice the cab" she said.

The inspector returned to the constable and asked if he had discovered the phone or anything else, but the constable nodded.

"Come," the inspector instructed Johnny, and they proceeded to the north entrance.

"We discovered Sakshi's body here," the inspector said.

"Yes, sir!" the constable exclaimed.

"What is your opinion, Johnny?"

"I concur with the doctor. It's the Perigoso," the constable stated.

"You've been here since you were a child; have you ever seen that dead bodies are found more than once a year?" the inspector asked.

Johnny nodded in no.

"This is where the perpetrator erred. That bastard will be behind bars soon." The inspector's confidence oozed from his words.

"Send the body to forensics and find out about that cab and the driver," the inspector ordered, staring at the Perigoso.

Everyone came to Priyanka's house. Priyanka was lost in Garima's memories while sitting on a couch in the drawing room. Atul was sitting on a bean bag to the left of Priyanka; Armaan and Sahil were sitting on the other couch; and Poonish was standing behind Atul. They were all quiet, but the silence was murmuring.

"I never thought anything like this could happen to any of us," Arman said, breaking the silence.

"She was the strongest among all of us," Sahil said.

"It hasn't been long since I arrived at this family, but with Garima, it seemed as if I had known her for a long time." Poonish described her as caring and kind.

"She loved me like her little brother," Atul said, starting to weep.

After seeing Atul, Priyanka's flood of tears started flowing again, which she had stopped very hard.

She didn't want to expose her feelings to anyone else, so she stood up and went to her bedroom.

Her predicament was not seen by Poonish, so he followed her to the bedroom.

"Please leave me alone," Priyanka said sobbingly.

"I'm not going anywhere," Poonish said, sitting alongside her and holding her hand.

"She was my mom, my dad, my everything." "How will I live now?" she said.

"I understand how you feel right now." He spoke.

"I would never have let her go if I had known that this would happen to her." "I don't want to live," Priyanka said.

"Shh! Don't say this. It is easy to die for someone, but it's hard to live." Poonish tried to comfort her by saying, "Life goes on, and we have to adjust ourselves according to life, and for you, we're all here." He caressed her shoulder to console her, but Priyanka's sobs didn't stop.

Everyone's emotional fortitude increased a little bit throughout the day. Sahil, Atul, and Arman were conversing while sitting down and talking at night. Poonish emerged from Priyanka's room carrying a glass of half-filled orange juice.

Poonish joined them and remarked, "Finally, she is sleeping. "It will take her a long time to recover from all this."

"One of us has to stay with her all the time," Arman said.

"I just want that fucking bastard, then I'll show him hell," Sahil said in a vengeful statement.

"We all want to capture her, but now Priyanka is our priority," Arman remarked.

"And the inspector knows his duty very well," Poonish added.

"I think we should all stay here for tonight, then we'll decide who will stay with Priyanka and when," Atul suggested.

They all agreed to it. The night grew dark. Sleep was standing at the door, but everyone was so engrossed in their thoughts that no one opened the door.

When the sun was yawing in the early morning. Shahzad headed to the lab. He was tense, so he straightaway went to Dr Chauhan's cabin, but there was no one there. He inquired about where the doctor was. He was told that the doctor was on the terrace. Shazaad swiftly reached the terrace. Where the cool morning breeze blew. The doctor stood there, looking up at the sky, as though waiting for the sun to rise.

"What are you doing here?" Shahzad asked.

"For the questions for which you have come here, I am also looking for answers to those questions here," the doctor said.

Shahzad approached him, and, like him, he began staring at the sky.

"What did the corpse say?" Shahzad asked.

"Blood clotting. The blood has thickened to the point where the heart can no longer pump it. Buries were made as a result of this," the doctor explained.

Shahzad felt relieved that the cause of death had been determined. But before he could rejoice, the doctor shattered his hopes by saying, "But."

"What drives me crazy is that her blood has turned black. Because of which all her veins and arteries have become black. This circumstance is nearly unthinkable in science. I have all my books and experiences on one side, and on the other side are the cases of Perigoso," the doctor said.

Hearing all this, a storm of questions arose in the inspector's mind, but not a single word came out of his mouth.

The doctor placed his hand on Shahzad's shoulder and said, "I hope you understand this case and the previous one," and went downstairs.

The inspector couldn't understand anything at that time. The sun came up, but the enigma deepened.

The Third And The Fourth Chase

Shahzad arrived at the police station after meeting with the doctor. His vision was filled with despondency. He walked to his cabin and summoned Johnny.

"Good morning, sir!" Johnny saluted.

"Good morning," the inspector said less enthusiastically.

"Do you get any information about the cab or the driver?" the inspector inquired.

"Not quite yet, sir!" Johnny responded.

"We don't have a lot of time. I don't know how, but I want the driver right here in two days." The inspector gave the ultimatum.

Johnny gave a nod.

"Have you gotten anything from Garima's post-mortem report?" the constable asked.

Shahzad inhaled deeply. "No! "The doctor just repeated the same old tale."

"You've been here for 7 years, and you still think it's just a story," Johnny pointed out.

"I know this town's history, but I also know the difference between real and being real," Shahzad said.

Johnny's look indicated that he disagreed with this assertion, but as a junior, he couldn't correct Shahzad.

"We are the only ones who can help ourselves." Shahzad said, and he ordered Johnny to bring him all the files in which Perigoso had been mentioned in the previous 5 years.

On the other hand, at Priyanka's house. They all agreed that Arman would stay at home with Priyanka for the day while the others would run the gallery.

Everyone was working hard, whether at the police station or in the gallery. Hours flew by like minutes. When the sunlight turned to moonlight, Johnny entered the cabin. He saw that the cabin was messy, that files were strewn around, and that the inspector was lost among them.

"Sir!" he exclaimed, distracting the inspector.

"I told you I don't want to have lunch," Shahzad remarked, his face flushed.

"But sir! It's time for dinner now," Johnny said.

Shahzad flabbergasted and looked at his wrist watch.

"What the fuck! "The more I move forward, the more I fall behind," the inspector grumbled, clutching his head.

"You should unwind." Johnny stated, "Only a clam mind can think."

Shahzad was fatigued, so he agreed to Johnny, but he kept the files with him.

Atul and Sahil were set to depart the gallery after completing their work. They both approached Poonish and asked whether he had completed his work or not. Poonish told them to leave because he had some work and the deadline was tomorrow.

"Okay, then, see you tomorrow," Sahil said.

"Take care," Atul said.

"You too," Poonish said.

They got outside, and Sahil started his bike, with Atul sitting behind him. Both had left and were passing through Perigoso. Suddenly, Sahil saw his 12-year-old sister standing at the north entrance, and seeing Sahil, she hurried into the forest. Sahil immediately stopped on the bike, causing them to stagger. Sahil took control of the bike and shouted Roohi! (Sahil's sister's name).

"What happen?" Atul asked.

They both dismount the bike.

"Roohi has gone to the Perigoso," Sahil remarked a little uneasily.

"Roohi and here. It's just your illusion," Atul said.

"I have just seen with my eyes," Sahil was convincing him.

"How can she be here? Bro, it's Perigoso, and you know it," Atul stated.

Sahil's thought was not agreeable, but Atul's words were right, so they sat back on the bike.

All of a sudden, a voice came from the forest, "Sahil bhaiya."

"Listen! Is this still an illusion? I'm going in." Sahil remarked as he handed Atul the bike keys.

"Wait," said Atul. He was too scared to go inside, but because of their years of friendship, he said, "I'll come with you."

They came in through the northern entrance. They were searching everywhere, shouting her name loudly. They were on a search together, but they couldn't find her. As a result, they decided to split up and search in different directions. The moon was obscured by clouds.

Atul was slowly moving forward. He was so terrified that he was fearful of even a moving branch of a tree, and when he tried to shout "roohi", his voice trembled. He moved deeper into the forest.

Suddenly he noticed someone behind a tree. He shouted, "Roohi, are you there?" but received no response. So, he proceeded carefully towards the tree. When he arrived, he discovered that there was no young girl there but rather a man.

To find out, he tapped the man's shoulder. The man turned around; it was Poonish with his eyes closed.

"Ohh! Poonish, thank God it's you..." Atul got relaxed but in the next second, "Wait for a second, but you said you had important work," he became suspicious.

Poonish was mumbling something, then the clouds parted and the moon shone brightly. Then Poonish opened his eyes, which were bloody-red.

"Hello, my friend," Poonish said in a deep tone as he stood in Atul's shadow.

"You are not Poonish," Atul said fearfully as he sought to flee Poonish, but he couldn't move an inch.

"I'm the Imperious!" Poonish laughed loudly.

Atul tried everything, but when he realised, he couldn't move from there, he sat down on his knees and said, "Please... Let me go, I beg you. I came here by mistake," he sobbed.

"Atul, you are so naïve,"

"That's why I've given you 5 minutes; if you can get out of this forest in those 5 minutes, you'll be safe and alive. But! "If you can't, then you'll meet your friend Garima," Poonish said.

Atul was at a loss on what to do.

"My friend, the time is ticking," Poonish said, pointing to his wrist watch.

Atul began running, his only thought being to escape out of the forest, so he ran as fast as he could. It was a race between life and death for him. He couldn't see a route because there were so many big trees around him. He came to a halt, and his breathing became violent. A thought flashed in his mind; he closed his eyes to concentrate on listening. Various sounds filled the forest, yet his focus was unwavering. He eventually heard the sound of an automobile engine and fled in that direction.

After ran a bit he was overjoyed to see the way out and was ready to step out of the forest, but suddenly he let out a sigh and his back began to bleed. He staggered back, but no one was there, not even his shadow. Poonish was still standing on Atul's shadow in the forest, stabbing it with a knife. He did it about five times.

"Did I mention that there are no rules in this game?" Poonish exclaimed, terribly laughing.

Atul died on the spot, and his body was lying at the south-east entrance.

On the other hand, Sahil was still looking for his sister.

"Roohi, roohi," he shouted.

"Bahiya," a sound came from behind him. He turned around and saw Roohi.

"What are you doing here? Does Dad know you're here?" Sahil chastised her.

Roohi was deafeningly silent.

"Now, let's go home," he remarked and walked towards her.

His phone suddenly rang, and it was his father's call. "Look, dad is calling, idiot," he remarked as he picked up the phone.

"Hello! Where are you, Bhaiya? We're waiting for you; come quickly," Roohi said from the other end of the phone call.

Sahil was taken aback, and his phone tumbled on the ground.

He remembered Atul's remarks: "It's just your illusion". He understood that something was fishy. So, he shouted, "Atul…. Atul."

Roohi, who was in front of him, was laughing loudly.

"You ……. Who the hell are you? Where is Atul?" he asked aggressively.

The girl extended her right hand, which was clutching a flower. She blew on the flower, causing all of its petals to fall into Sahil's shadow.

"Permutador," she said, and the petals all vanished into the shadow.

"Innocent Atul is at peace with Garima," the girl smirked.

Sahil's rage was boiling over. He wanted to step forward and kill that girl, but he couldn't lift his legs. His feet appeared to be stuck to the ground.

"What happened, Bhaiya?" she emphasised on bhaiya to provoke him.

"You bitch," Sahil's face went blazing red with rage.

"You shouldn't have said to me this; now that he's awake, he won't let you live." She closed her eyes.

"Who the fuck is he now?" Sahil exclaimed.

"The Imperious," she replied solemnly, opening her crimson eyes.

Sahil was still staring at her fumingly.

"Queridos fihos," she said, as thousands of insects, some flying, some crawling, and others walking, surrounded Sahil.

Sahil was aghast to see this.

"Say hello to your friends," she said and snapped her fingers.

All the insects swooped down on him. He panicked and continued to try to extract the insects from his body, but it was futile. Insects were biting him and sucking his blood, and he screamed in agony.

After a minute, the girl snapped her fingers once more, and all the insects went away. Sahil died after collapsing to the ground.

"Quarto," the girl said, smiling.

Shahzad was so engrossed in the files by this point that he began to get a headache. As a result, he took a pill and went to bed. Sleep overtook him as soon as he lay down on the bed. But his hard day was not over yet; his phone rang.

"Hello" he picked up but he was in sleep.

"Sir! Two more corpses were found from the Perigoso," Johnny said from the other end of the phone call.

"What?" Shahzad said as he awoke from his slumber.

"Yes sir," Johnny said.

"I'll be there in 20 minutes," Shahzad said in disappointment.

Shahzad rushed out of the house, forgetting to change his clothing and leaving in his nightgown.

A disagreement broke out between his heart and his mind on the way. While his mind insisted that there was some vicious person behind all this, his heart insisted that Perigoso's story was true.

He arrived at the spot exactly in 20 minutes. First, Johnny led him to the third entrance (south-east), where he saw Atul's corpse. He used a torch to thoroughly examine Atul's back. There was only blood on the back, but there were no wounds.

The inspector was once again perplexed.

"The other one," Shahzad asked.

Johnny led Shahzad 500 metres ahead to the fourth entrance (south-west).

"Again, the entrance," the inspector said.

They saw Sahil's corpse. On which the ants were roaming. There were several bite marks on the body. Whenever the blood was spilled, ants were roaming on it too. They both didn't conclude anything.

The inspector's phone rang again, this time from the commissioner.

"Jay Hind, sir!" he said as he picked up the phone.

"What are you doing? Dead bodies are being found one after the other in your area," the commissioner chastised.

"Sir! "I'm straining every nerve," the inspector said.

"Okay! "Then tell me how far your investigation has progressed and who the culprit is," the commissioner said.

"There is no culprit," Shahzad said.

"What rubbish,"

"Sir! It's the Perigoso." Shahzad's heart triumphed over his mind.

"Shut up! Make no excuses for your procrastination. You have proven my decision to be wrong. You can't bear the pressure of this case right now. I am giving you a week off, and then you'll join the traffic," the commissioner said.

"But sir," Shahzad was interrupted by the Commissioner, "it's an order."

"Okay sir! Jay hind" Shahzad hung up the phone. He was so enraged that he threw his phone on the road and drove away.

The Super Cop

In Ratlam, Madhya Pradesh, at a police station. Everyone looked fresh, like the first ray of the morning. A sub-inspector walked in. He was 32 years old. He had a twinkle in his eyes. The name Ankit Sharma flashed brightly on his badge. Everyone in the station saluted him. After that, he approached Pawan Bhadouriya, a constable who was reading the newspaper.

"Sir! You are all over the news these days because you solved the triple murder case," the constable said, placing the newspaper on the table.

"I don't want fame," the SI stated before taking a seat at the table.

"Why so, sir!" the constable asked.

"Fames comes with a lot of criticism, and once you get caught up in it, it's difficult to get even a peaceful morning tea," the SI said and the landline began to ring "as I said."

The call was answered by Constable.

"Sir, someone is terrified and wants to talk to you," the constable said as he handed Ankit the phone.

"SI Ankit is speaking,"

"My son has been kidnapped," a man on the other end of the line stated.

"Be calm and tell me everything," Ankit said.

"His name is Sourabh and he is 17 years old. Sir! He used to go for a morning walk every day, but today he went for a walk but didn't return. We received a call from a kidnapper demanding a 5-lakh ransom," the man said.

Ankit was paying close attention to him. The man's voice had an echo to it.

"Where are you talking from?" Ankit asked.

"They know all our movements, so I came in the bathroom," the man replied.

"Don't panic; I'll be there," Ankit remarked as he hung up the phone.

"Bhadouriya ji, let's have a cup of tea," Ankit proposed to the constable.

The constable ordered tea.

"Sir! It's an average case; can I take this case?" the constable said.

Ankit drank a sip. He grew overjoyed and exclaimed, "Cardamon and ginger!" The best combination in tea."

The constable was staring at him, waiting for his answer.

"Yes! Without a doubt. Just give me the first hour, and the rest is up to you," Ankit remarked, glancing at him.

"You always say that and solve the case in the first hour,"

Ankit burst out laughing.

Ankit called the man exactly 10 minutes later and asked if he had received a call from the kidnapper.

"No, sir!" the man replied.

"Is there a back door, window, or something in your house that only you know about?" Ankit asked.

"Yes! "There's a window," the man said.

"Superb! Just send me your location," Ankit said, hanging up the phone. "Bhadouriya ji, take out the jeep. I'll be coming".

"What was the point of waiting for 10 minutes when he had to leave?" The constable inquired, perplexed.

"I had to confirm whether the kidnapers are actually keeping an eye on them or not." Ankit stated.

"Superb!" the constable exclaimed.

"Shall we go now," Ankit said.

Ankit arrived immediately, dressed casually, and they both left the police station, but they turned off the jeep's siren.

Ankit got out of the vehicle 800 metres away from the man's house and said, "Listen, keep driving the Jeep for 700 to 1200 metres in this area. Don't stop until I say so. Maintain a modest speed and turn on the siren. Is that clear?" Ankit ordered the constable

"Yes, sir!" the constable exclaimed while following Ankit's instructions. Ankit, on the other hand, approached the back window with caution, where the man and his wife awaited him.

"How many windows are there on the ground floor?" Ankit asked from the outside.

"Two," the man replied.

"Cover both windows with curtains simultaneously," Ankit instructed.

The man and his wife covered the windows. Ankit entered the house from the back window.

"Where is your son's bedroom?" Ankit asked.

"Come sir!" the man said.

They went up to the first floor and stood at the door. The man's phone abruptly rang. It was the kidnapper's phone call. He picked up the phone and turned on the speaker. The kidnapper asked him why he put the curtains up and told him to take them down. Ankit was paying close attention to the phone call.

Ankit instructed the man to pull back the curtains.

The man walked downstairs, untied all the curtains, and returned to Ankit.

"Does this room have a window?" Ankit asked.

"There is one," the man replied.

"You know what to do," Ankit said.

The man entered and closed the window curtain. Ankit then entered the room and began scanning it. Everything in the room was well arranged. There were also several books by Sherlock Holmes, Byomkesh Bakshi, and Chanakya Niti. The man's phone rang again. It was the kidnapper again. They threatened the man that they would kill his son if the curtains were pulled again on the window. Ankit hid in a corner and told the man to take down the drapes. The man pulled back the curtains.

"Don't look at me, just listen. You will call someone and speak with him for 30 to 40 seconds. When the kidnapper calls, you'll tell them that you are arranging the money," Ankit described the plan.

It went exactly as Ankit had planned. The kidnapper had called. The same thing was said by the man. Ankit was paying close attention and heard the sound of a police siren in the call. Ankit motioned for the man to go downstairs and soon called the constable.

"Where are you? Ankit asked.

"In the H block?" the constable replied.

Ankit closed his eyes and mentally mapped out the entire H block. He was so engaged in his thoughts that he appeared to have arrived at H block. He was inspecting every street, every house, and even every corner when his gaze was drawn to a now-dilapidated school. He instantly opened his eyes and questioned the constable, "Are you near the school?"

"Yes sir!" the constable replied.

"They're in the school, and they're watching you right now, so just distract them, and I'll be there in a few minutes," Ankit explained.

Bhadouriya stepped out of the jeep and walked to the school gate. He was yawing and passing the time by walking one or two steps and glancing around. Meanwhile, Ankit approached the school in secret with that man and his wife.

"Wait here," Ankit said as he jumped from the school playground's wall. He immediately rushed to the terrace, where he covertly noticed an 18-year-old boy with binoculars. He called the constable and told him to bring the man and his wife into the school. Then Ankit approached the boy, slapped him twice, yanked his hair, and asked, "Where is Sourabh?"

"I don't know," the terrified boy said.

"You must have known me, because if you play this 'don't know' game, I'll throw you from here," Ankit snarled.

"8th C, 2nd floor," the boy stuttered.

When the constable arrived, Ankit was bringing that boy downstairs. Ankit handed over the boy to the constable, and then they all went to the 8th C. Where they all saw two more boys with knives in their hands, and Sourabh was tied to a chair with a rope.

"If anybody is planning to flee the room, keep in mind that the bullet is faster than you," Ankit said.

Sourabh was untied and caressed by the man and his wife.

The constable arrested the three lads and was about to take them away when Ankit stopped him and instructed him to take the main culprit with him.

Everyone was perplexed.

"Sourabh, the longer you wait for the truth, the longer you'll be in jail," the inspector said.

Everyone was totally flabbergasted to hear this.

"Sir! What are you saying," the man said.

Ankit ignored the man's words and fixed his gaze on Sourabh.

"Yes! It's me," Sourabh said.

On the one hand, the parents were enraged, but on the other, they felt helpless.

"I don't want to be with you both. You're always fighting. I don't remember us ever sitting together as a family. I just want moments of peace. When I got the money, I would have left right away. That's why I devised this plan," Sourabh said.

The parents exchanged glances, remained mute, and their eyes were filled with shame.

"Parenting isn't about providing only basic needs. Parents are the ones who offer their children direction, affection, and other things. I'm not filing this case, but it's your responsibility to make sure he doesn't do this again," Ankit said.

The parents accepted their fault. Sourabh was curious to know how Ankit cracked his plan, so he asked, but Ankit just passed him a smile and said, "Rethink your plan; the answer is there."

Ankit's phone rang again.

"Hello," Ankit said as he answered the phone.

"How are you, my champ?" Goa's commissioner was on the other side of the call.

"I'm doing very well, sir, and it's all because of you," Ankit said, his face brightening with a smile.

"Come to Goa; I need you in a very typical case," the commissioner said.

"The forest case," Ankit said solemnly.

"Finish your remaining work as soon as possible and come here. I'll take care of all the formalities. Because this is a dangerous case, I advise you not to bring the family with you." The commissioner hung up the phone.

Ankit appeared solemn at the time.

The Decision

One month had passed since Atul's and Sahil's death. Priyanka no longer visited the gallery. She decided to leave Goa and move to her uncle's place in Mumbai, as this house held Garima's memories that used to bring her to tears. She wanted to move on with her life, which she couldn't do by staying here.

The gallery had been run by Arman and Poonish. They could have employed more personnel, but people had ceased visiting the gallery. Only a few selected customers used to come. The season of happiness in these three lives appeared to be over. Also, there was no one in charge of this case, so Johnny's interest in it began to wane. With these four deaths, the public's fear of Perigoso grew.

The relaxing Sunday began with a sweltering morning. On the one hand, Ankit boarded a flight from Raja Bhoj airport to Goa, while on the other hand, Arman arrived at Poonish's house.

Poonish opened the gate.

"Hey," Poonish exclaimed, surprised to see Arman, "come."

Arman entered, and Poonish escorted him to the drawing room, where he sat on the couch.

"Is everything okay?" Poonish asked.

"If I look back at the last few months, I'm not doing well." Arman expressed his dissatisfaction.

"When I moved from Delhi, Sahil was the first one to help me establish the gallery. Then Garima, Priyanka, and Atul came, and after that you. Those were the fragments of my heart."

"I can understand your feelings," Poonish said in low energy.

"I've never missed my family in these six years, but now I can't stand it. I'm moving to Delhi," Arman said.

Arman drew an envelope from his pocket and put it on the table. "Your salary; I'm selling the gallery," he lamented.

Poonish wanted to ask Arman why he was doing this, but he couldn't because he saw the sorrow in Arman's eyes. It was agonising for both of them. Then Arman stood up and embraced Poonish.

"Take care, and keep in touch," Poonish said.

"You too, and one more thing: Priyanka is also moving to Mumbai, to her uncle's house. I think you should also meet her for one last time." Arman smiled, but only pain could be seen in his smile, and he left.

That was Poonish's second shocking piece of news. As lovely as the morning had been, it had suddenly turned completely unpleasant for Poonish. He promptly picked up the keys and went to Priyanka's house. He was finally driving Chinki after a long time. After arriving at Priyanka's house, he rang the doorbell.

To see Priyanka, it seemed sadness had snatched the light off her face. She invited Poonish inside, and the two sat down on the couches. Poonish looked around and noticed some cartons. The walls and to a lesser extent, the rooms were vacant. She appeared to have packed everything.

Poonish took a deep breath. "So, you've decided to move."

"The life that I can't imagine, but now I have to live it," she said.

"Everything is falling apart, and it's sometimes good to run away from your sorrow," she added.

Poonish recognised his words in Priyanka's statement. He remembered Sakshi's words at the time.

"When we are with family, we can easily handle any situation," he said, becoming more rational.

For 15 minutes, they were lost in each other's eyes. Despite the fact that they didn't say anything, their eyes told the entire story. The landline rang, breaking the never-ending silence.

Priyanka went to the other room to pick up the phone.

"Hello! Yes, uncle, yeah, packing is almost done. Until noon,"

Because there was silence in the house, Poonish could hear everything Priyanka said. Poonish became depressed after hearing all of the conversation. He assumed Priyanka had made her decision to depart, so he simply went without saying anything.

Priyanka finished the conversation and returned to the drawing room. Poonish wasn't present, but his bike keys were on the table.

Poonish was seated on a bench in a park half a mile from Priyanka's house. His heart was screaming at him, questioning why he didn't stop Priyanka from leaving. But he was quiet, as if sadness had paralysed him.

After a moment, his heart began to beat faster, as Priyanka came and sat next to him.

"You forgot your keys at my place," she said, handing him the keys.

"Thank you," he mumbled quietly.

"This place means a lot to me. Every Sunday, Mom, Dad, Garima, and I looked forward to coming here. I used to paint with mom, and Garima used to box with dad. It's strange; I'm leaving here, and today is also Sunday," Priyanka recalled her memories.

"Then don't go" the sorrow of separation obvious in his eyes. "You are the face of my future. You are one of the reasons I stayed here. At first, I thought it was just an attraction, but then I realised it was more than that. You're leaving, and it's agonising for me, but there's nothing I can't do."

The silence sat between them.

Priyanka pulled a stale lily bloom from her pocket and asked, "Do you remember this?"

Poonish agreed with a nod.

"I was given flowers by many people in school and collages, but I used to throw them all; I don't know why I can't throw this one. I used to like you, but once Sakshi died, you became a different person. On the one hand, you ignore me, and on the other hand, you look after me. I'm confused," she said.

"Let me simplify this for you," he said.

Poonish revealed his truth.

For more than 5 minutes, Priyanka was stunned.

Poonish closed his eyes. He felt that, like everyone else, Priyanka would also leave, and he couldn't see her leaving.

She returned the flower to her pocket and then rested her head on Poonish's shoulder.

Happiness kissed Poonish's face when he opened his eyes and saw this.

"Looks like I'll have to keep this flower for the rest of my life," she said.

The feeling of love blossoms between them.

Ankit landed in Goa by noon and headed straight to the police station. Everyone was surprised to see him, but they saluted him at the same time.

Johnny came to him and said, "Sir, your duty starts tomorrow."

"I like to be ahead of time," Ankit said "Mr....?"

Johnny introduced himself and led Ankit to his new cabin.

"You can unwind; I'll bring fresh kokum juice for you," Johnny said.

"Only juice," Ankit insists.

"Please tell me, sir! What do you want to eat?" Johnny asked.

"Case file," Ankit said.

Johnny gave him a startling look.

"I'm not used to repeating twice. Please hurry," Ankit said, his demeanour showing.

"Yes sir!" Johnny stammered and walked away.

On the other hand, Priyanka and Poonish arrived at the gallery. They opened the door, and Arman, who was packing his stuff on the ground floor, said, without looking at them, "The gallery is closed forever."

"The gallery can never be closed," Priyanka said with a smile.

Arman turned back, relieved to see them since there was a part of him that didn't want to leave. After all he had given himself six years to establish this gallery.

"We lost some of our family members. I know it's hard, but we have to take a fresh start," Poonish said. "So, Mr. Arman, are you ready to get back to your drawing board?"

Arman's eyes welled up with tears, and he nodded, hurried towards them, and embraced them.

At the police station, Ankit read the case file except for the post-mortem file since he believed the post-mortem report would create confusion. He studied all day but came up empty-handed. He was well aware that this was a difficult case to crack.

He called Johnny and asked him why there was no evidence, even though a statement was not recorded. The case didn't move an inch, and he asked whether he had found the driver or not.

Johnny was quiet, but his quietness answered no.

"If I don't get the driver in front of me by tomorrow evening, you'll join Shahzad and also summon all the persons who are related to this case." Ankit gave an ultimatum to Johnny and drank the fourth glass of kokum juice.

Finding The One

Ankit began his inquiry the next morning at the police station. First, he inquired about Sahil's and Atul's families. He then posed queries to Sakshi's boss. He then summoned Arman and Priyanka.

The investigation began with them in the dark room, where only a bulb was on. There were two chairs and a table. Arman and Priyanka sat on the seats, Ankit sat on the table in front of them, and Johnny stood behind the table.

"Priyanka! Had you noticed anything unusual about your sister's behaviour before that night?" Ankit asked.

"She didn't come with us for some days," Priyanka said after pondering.

"You never asked where she was going?" Ankit asked.

"She used to say she has some work. I thought there would be some work in the gallery," she said.

"No! Garima used to leave the gallery like everyone else. She despised overtime," Arman said.

"So, it's a possibility that she used to meet that boy," Ankit speculated.

"Did Garima take drugs?" Ankit asked.

"No! Never," Priyanka said, becoming offended.

"My questions are bitter, but they're for your benefit, like medicine," Ankit said calmly.

"Where were you on the night of Sahil's and Atul's murder?" he asked Arman.

"I was at Priyanka's house. Poonish, Atul, and Sahil were at the gallery," Arman replied.

"How long have you known both of them?" Ankit asked.

"Sahil for 6 years and Atul for 5 and a half years," Arman replied.

"If everyone knows the Perigoso's story, then why did they choose that path?" Ankit asked.

"It's a shortcut, and most people use it," Arman explained.

"Thank you for your cooperation," Ankit said as he finished his onslaught of questions.

He took a short break, and Johnny brought him kokum juice.

Ankit took a sip, "huh! Refreshing. "I think I'm in love with this juice."

"Sir! You've had this 10th glass of juice since morning," Johnny joked.

"Leave my juice alone and tell me who's up next," Ankit said.

"Poonish!" Johnny said.

"Called him in," Ankit sipped again.

Poonish entered and sat.

"You are popular in this case," Ankit said to Poonish.

"Sorry! I don't get you," Poonish remarked, glancing at Johnny and asking, "Where is Inspector Shahzad?"

"He loved the stories of this town so much; therefore, we sent him to Disney," Ankit laughed alone.

Johnny and Poonish exchanged serious glances.

"Okay! My bad," Ankit said. "Correct me if I'm wrong; you were the last person who was with Sakshi, Sahil, and Atul."

Poonish agreed with a nod.

"Tell me about your last encounter with your sister." Ankit asked.

"We were in the kitchen. Sakshi was cooking, and I was chopping veggies. I fainted unexpectedly, and the next morning we found her body," Poonish explained.

"And with Sahil and Atul?" Ankit asked.

"We were working at the gallery as usual. They finished their work and came to ask whether I had finished as well, but I had some papers to file, so I instructed them to leave, and the next morning we found their lifeless bodies," Poonish explained.

"How long have you been in Goa?" Ankit asked.

"8 months," Poonish replied.

Ankit urged Poonish to go once he finished questioning him. Then Ankit and Johnny returned to the cabin.

"Sir! "I had already told you they didn't know anything," Johnny said.

Ankit was deep in contemplation. "Poonish and Perigoso. These two are linked to every death. All of Poonish's claims are moonshines, and Perigoso has something," he whispered.

"I want every single detail about Poonish," Ankit ordered Johnny. "And I have to check the Perigoso," he said to himself.

They both exited the police station and proceeded to their respective destinations. Johnny went to the cab companies, and Ankit went to the Perigoso.

Ankit arrived at the Perigoso, got out of the jeep, and attentively examined the forest. 'The culprit called the four victims into the woods, killed them, and left them at the entrance. So that people believe the Perigoso is behind everything.' He concluded after inspecting the four entrances from which the corpses were discovered.

He took the decision to enter the woodland. He heard a whistle as he was about to enter through the northern entrance. When he turned around, he saw that it was Poonish.

"Think of the devil, and the devil will appear," Ankit said in jest.

"I concur with you," Poonish said in a deep tone, and his face lit up with the same wicked smile.

"Are you following me?" Ankit asked.

"Maybe, maybe not," Poonish replied.

"I have a gut feeling that you are behind all of this," Ankit stated as he approached Poonish.

"You are sagacious," Poonish smiled.

"And you pretend to be innocent"

"Tell me everything; otherwise, I have many ways," Ankit said.

Poonish closed his eyes and drew a cool breath before opening his red eyes and saying, "I'm eager to see them."

Ankit was astounded to see that, but then he calmed himself.

"Sombra," Poonish said, seeing Ankit's shadow.

Ankit looked around, but nothing happened.

Poonish then yelled "sombra," but again nothing happened. His body language had changed, and he became perplexed. Then Ankit grabbed his collar and said, "Now it's my turn."

Suddenly, a black butterfly landed on his hand, and just then the Perigoso was enveloped in fog. Ankit turned around, and in the meantime, Poonish kicked him, causing Ankit to fall face down in the forest.

"How dare you", Ankit's anger reached its peak. He dashed towards Poonish, but an invisible wall stopped him at the entrance. He was dumbfounded by all this. He threw several punches and kicks in an attempt to escape, but all were futile.

"What the fuck!" Ankit shouted.

Poonish waved goodbye and began reciting the spell.

"Eu invoco a morte,

"Do subterraneo mais escuro"

The effect of magic began. The fog had turned into poisonous black smoke. Ankit began coughing; his eyes were burning, and tears streamed from them. Saliva began to flow from his mouth. He began to suffocate gradually. His condition was deteriorating.

"Para aumentar seu…"

Suddenly, Poonish got a shock and his spell broke. The black smoke and the invisible wall vanished. Ankit passed out and collapsed at the entrance. Poonish yelled fumingly; his gaze fixed on the sky.

On the other hand, Johnny was inquiring about the driver. He asked the manager for a list of all the drivers employed by that company. After waiting for a while, he received the list. He was looking at it carefully when he received a call from the hospital. He left the list after attending the call and rushed to the hospital.

When he arrived at the hospital, he asked the receptionist, "where is the inspector?"

"1st floor, ward no. 5," the receptionist replied.

He hurried to the ward and waited for the doctor to emerge.

The doctor eventually emerged.

"What happened?" Johnny asked.

"He was having a panic attack. Now, he is no longer in danger. He'll be conscious soon," the doctor said.

"From where did you find him?" Johnny asked.

"He brought him here," said the doctor, motioning to a boy sitting on a bench.

Johnny approached the boy and asked him where he found Ankit.

"When I was passing through Perigoso, I saw the inspector lying fainting at the entrance. Then I quickly brought him here. Perhaps he had gone into the woods," the boy said.

Johnny was flabbergasted to hear this, but he thanked that boy and came into Ankit's room. He was concerned about Ankit.

Ankit regained consciousness after 2 hours. He was quite surprised to find himself in the hospital. When he noticed Johnny sitting beside him, he asked him, "How am I here?"

Johnny was relieved to see Ankit awake.

"This question I think I have to ask you," Johnny said, "what were you doing in the Perigoso?"

Ankit was attempting to recall what had happened to him, but he couldn't.

"I was going to inspect the Perigoso, then I... I 'don't know what happened to me," Ankit said.

"You are new here, but I have lived here since I was a child, and I assure you that this is not just a story." Johnny stated.

"You again," Johnny interrupted Ankit. "Please listen to me; this isn't the first time we've discovered bodies from the Perigoso. This murder spree has been going on for 111 years; the only difference this time is that we discovered four dead in just six months. Sir, please! Keep your scrunty away from the Perigoso," Johnny warned before leaving Ankit to rest.

Ankit completely ignored everything Johnny said. He was considering things from a different angle. He considered that his investigation was on the right path. The criminal understood this, which is why culprit did everything he could, to distract him.

"I'll kill that bastard," he said confidently.

Ankit was discharged after a day and returned to his duties, full of beans.

Arman sat at the counter in the gallery, reviewing the stock list, while Poonish arranged products for the shelves. The gallery had not yet opened. They were working while having a casual discussion.

Poonish noticed Arman's shadow was in front of him. The devil suddenly opened his crimson eyes and stood in the shadows. He began to recite his spell.

"Eu invoco a morte,

"Do subterraneo mais escuro"

Arman coughed and drank from the water bottle. His stomach began to ache as a result. He didn't pay much attention at first because the pain was minor, but it gradually increased. He felt something in his stomach. So, he rolled up his t-shirt and noticed a black shoe mark on his belly. He panicked and screamed in pain, causing him to fall from the chair. Fortunately, his shadow moved from the floor to the wall.

This shocked Poonish and broke his spell. He, too, stumbled backward. Meanwhile, Priyanka walked into the gallery. She noticed Poonish on the ground on one side and Arman mumbling on the other. She first picked up Poonish, and then they both picked up Arman. Priyanka handed water to Arman and inquired, "What happened?"

Arman recounted the entire experience and removed his t-sh0irt to show them the shoe mark, but the mark had vanished by then. Priyanka and Poonish exchanged glances. Fear could be seen in their eyes.

The Fifth Chase

Johnny got some vital facts regarding Poonish. So, he was telling Ankit about it at the police station.

"Sir! Poonish is a strange character. Because he doesn't stay in one place for long, no one knows much about him. I looked for his documents on the official website, but there was no ID card. Nobody knows anything about his parents, either. Sakshi was a cousin of his, not his real sister."

Ankit pondered for a moment before saying, "Let's go."

"Where?" Johnny asked.

"To know about his eight months in Goa," Ankit stated as they walked towards Poonish's neighbourhood.

There was an old woman who lived next door to Poonish. In that house, she lived alone. Her husband died a long time ago, and her daughter was in Denmark.

Ankit and Johnny approached her. She was seated on a chair in her yard, enjoying her morning tea.

"Sorry to bother you, mam, but we need to ask you some questions," Ankit said humbly.

"Of course! "Please take a seat," the old woman urged.

"Thank you," Ankit said as he sat on the chair.

"Tea?" the old woman offered, but they respectfully declined.

Ankit inquired her about Sakshi.

"Sakshi was a lovely and diligent girl. She reminded me of my daughter. She has been here for over a decade. She used to take care of me whenever I was sick. When Poonish came to stay here, she was overjoyed," the old woman informed Ankit.

"And what about Poonish?" Ankit inquired.

"He is an introvert with a pure heart. To say he was a younger brother who used to take care of Sakshi like a big brother."

"Can you tell me what happened that night? Did you see anyone else besides Poonish and Sakshi?" Ankit inquired.

"No! "As far as I recall, there were only those two," the old woman said.

"Did you notice any difference in Poonish after Sakshi's death?" Ankit inquired.

"Inspector, you know how difficult it is to recover when we lose someone. Poonish too succumbed to grief. But I want to thank that girl who looked after Poonish during his difficult times," the elderly woman remarked.

A wave of enthusiasm came on the withered faces of Ankit and Johnny when they heard this.

"How did she look?" Ankit inquired promptly.

"She was around 27–28, the same height as mine, and she had short burgundy hair," the old woman explained.

Johnny immediately showed her Garima's picture and asked, "Was that it?"

"Yes!" The old woman exclaimed.

"Did you see her on the night of May 12th with Poonish?" Ankit inquired.

"Sorry inspector, I wasn't here that night," the old woman explained.

Ankit thanked the old woman for her time. Then they questioned people at every surrounding residence. They left no stone unturned to find out whether Garima was with Poonish on May 12th, but they couldn't. Ankit felt relieved to have made the first move in this case.

They were then on their way to meet with a Chinese fast-food vendor who had notified the police about Sahil's and Atul's deaths. They drove through Perigoso and were at the van in an hour.

After seeing them, the vendor said, "What would you like to have, sir?"

"Just answers," Ankit said.

"But I have told you everything," the vendor pointed out to Johnny.

"I have some fresh questions," Ankit continued, "did you see anyone other than those two guys?"

The vendor shrugged and began washing the counter.

"Johnny! Let's take him to the police station and question him on our way. I assure you, he will remember everything," Ankit said with a chuckle.

Johnny advanced.

"Sir…...Sir! I tell you, "The vendor, terrified.

Johnny came to a standstill.

"Not with them, but after 20 minutes I saw a man who went into the Perigoso," the vendor hesitantly explained.

The statement came as a surprise to them.

"Why didn't you tell us this earlier?" Johnny chastised him.

"It was my anniversary, and my wife had made plans for the night. If I had told you everything, you would have stopped me until the morning," the vendor explained.

"You…" Johnny wanted to speak more, but his phone began to ring. He picked up the phone and drove a little further away.

"Do you remember his face?" Ankit inquired.

"Not much because it was quite dark," the vendor explained.

Johnny approached Ankit with a smile and said, "sir! We've got the driver."

This was like rain in a desert for Ankit. "Now, everything is under control."

"Call the driver to the police station, Ankit instructed. Come along with us and help us sketch whatever you remember about the guy," he told the vendor.

They were about to leave with the vendor when Ankit became dizzy and stumbled. Johnny held him and made him sit on the chair.

"You're still frail. You should go home and rest," Johnny advised Ankit.

"I'm fine," Ankit responded.

"Your health is more important than the case. I handle everything," Johnny explained.

"Okay!", Ankit reluctantly agreed to Johnny's request.

Then Johnny dropped Ankit off at his motel because Ankit had stayed there before going to the police station with the vendor.

Ankit took the medication and went to bed. Sleep had him in it arms in less than a minute. He awoke feeling refreshed after a four-hour nap. Outside, it was dark, and streetlights loomed over the roads. He checked his phone and found seven texts from Johnny and a missed call from his wife.

He began by reading the message.

"Sir! Poonish is the culprit; you are right. The driver left Garima off at Poonish's house, and the vendor says that he saw Poonish enter the Perigoso." These lines were written in the message.

He then dialled his wife's number.

"Hello," his wife said as she answered the phone.

"How are you?" he said.

"Why don't you pick up when I call?"

"I was a little busy," he explained.

"After going to Goa, you've become extremely busy. Are you focusing on the case or something else?" his wife inquired.

Ankit laughed.

"When are you going to return?" she asked.

"The case is closed, so the day after tomorrow," he added, "I'll bring you kokum juice. It is good for a pregnant woman."

"I'll be waiting," she said.

"Call you later, Bye," he said.

"I love you," she said.

"I love you too," he added as he hung up the phone.

The same enthusiasm returned to his face, which had been lost somewhere in Goa. On his approached to Poonish's place, he took his gun and sent a message to Priyanka. 'Come to Poonish's house with Arman,' he wrote.

He arrived in a matter of minutes. In his drawing room, Poonish was reading a book. When the doorbell rang, Poonish opened it. He was surprised to see the inspector and asked, "Did something happen, inspector?"

Ankit walked in without being invited.

"I've come here for your friends," Ankit said.

"I don't get you," Poonish said as he shut the door.

"Don't act innocent in front of me," Ankit remarked, taking out the handcuffs. "You're under arrest."

"For what?" Poonish was flabbergasted.

"I'm in charge of killing your cousin Sakshi, girlfriend Garima, and friends Atul and Sahil," Ankit said.

"Are you insane? You know nothing about me or this case. I think you should be sent to Disney instead of Shahzad," Poonish grumbled.

Ankit moved in closer to Poonish, clutching his collar. "I have proof, you dumas," he said before handcuffing Poonish.

They both exchanged scowls as though they were arch-enemies. The doorbell rang again, and this time it was rung by Priyanka and Arman.

"Gussets have arrived," Ankit remarked, attempting to open the door but failing.

"Open it, you idiot," Ankit said, but Poonish remained silent, his head lowered.

Priyanka was ringing the bell again and again.

"Wait a minute!" Ankit said, expecting both of them to hear him, but this did not happen.

"They can't hear you," Poonish said in a deep tone, raising his head. He transformed into a devil with red eyes. Ankit had seen the devil before, but he couldn't recall the previous encounter.

Priyanka and Arman left the door and went onto the lawn, worried about Poonish. There were two windows on the lawn, one for the drawing room and one for the kitchen. Windows were typically 5'7 in height. As they approached the drawing room window, they noticed Poonish was handcuffed and had red eyes.

They were unable to comprehend what was happening inside.

"Don't trick me." Ankit's rage was boiling over.

The handcuffs were broken as Poonish jerked his hands. Everyone was stunned when they saw that. Ankit's rage changed to terror.

"Jesus gave you a chance to save your life, but you blew it. I'm astounded that you survived as well, but now I'm not going to make any mistakes," Poonish stated.

Suddenly all four burners of the gas stove ignited. Poonish's face lit up with a devilish grin. This smile foreshadowed Ankit's demise.

Ankit was attempting to take his revolver, but he couldn't move since Poonish was standing in his shadow.

Priyanka was frozen as she watched all of this. Arman tried to go inside because this window was closed, so he walked to the kitchen window, which was also closed. Meanwhile, his gaze was drawn to the gas burners.

"Don't worry, I'll send juice to your pregnant wife." Poonish grinned.

As he thought about his wife and future child, Ankit's eyes welled up with tears. For the first time in his life, he felt sorry for himself for being an inspector.

"What the hell?" Arman dashed to the drawing room window, where he began shrieking and smashing the glass as he realised something fatal was about to happen. But when he realised it was a waste of time, he grasped Priyanka's hand and fled the house.

"Listen," Arman said in a trembling voice, while a destructive blast happened in the house. Arman and Priyanka were thrown to the ground as a result of the explosion. Poonish's house was engulfed in flames as a column of black smoke soared into the sky.

"POONISH," Priyanka screamed as loudly as she could. They dashed towards the house. Neighbours also gathered to hear the explosion. Because the flames were so high, no one was able to enter. Arman was concerned and Priyanka was crying.

After some time, the fire brigade and ambulance arrived. It took a significant amount of work to put out the fire. The firefighters proceeded inside the house, when the flames had died down a little after 15 minutes of hard work. After extensive searching, they discovered Poonish, who was naked, but no burn marks could be located on his body. Because he was breathing, they quickly wrapped his body in a cloth and carried him out. Poonish's survival pleased Priyanka and Arman. Poonish's body was kept in the ambulance.

Arman informed the firefighters that there was another person in the house, but the firefighters only spotted Poonish. To satisfy Arman, they once again went inside the house but didn't find anyone there. Arman felt very strange, but he still had something more important than Ankit. That's why he went to the hospital, sitting with Priyanka in the ambulance.

The Apprence Of Devil

It was midnight. The moon appeared brighter than before. The cool breeze added to the peacefulness of the forest. Everyone was resting peacefully in their homes. The storm began when the bodies of Sakshi, Garima, Atul, and Sahil vanished from the forensic lab. All of the bodies, including Ankit's, appeared at each entrance to the Perigoso.

Sakshi's body was at the north entrance.

Garima's body was at the northwest.

Atul's body was at the southwest.

Sahil's body was at the southeast.

Ankit's body was at the northeast.

Suddenly, a white light began to emanate from all of the corpses, forming a pattern that lit up the Perigoso. The white light created a seal around the Perigoso. A split second later, the seal broke and the earth began to tremble, causing a fissure between the road's edge and the Perigoso's edge. A swarm of black butterflies flew out of the forest, covering the entire sky.

Someone was exiting the Perigoso. He had crimson eyes that lacked an iris and a deathly pale face, as if he didn't have a drop of blood in his body. His hair was pulled back into a ponytail. He was dressed in a long, knee-length coat, a white linen shirt, and black pants. The shoes were gleaming.

Despite his gentlemanly attire, he was the devil. He didn't have a shadow. The grass dried out and turned black whenever he stepped on it.

He got out and stood on the road, taking a big breath and saying, "O mesmo velho vento" in a deep tone.

He looked around for a moment, then smiled wickedly.

"Let's take a look at my town," he said, and he proceeded ahead.

Everything had changed; where there had been huts, there were now new structures, and the crowded marketplaces had new and large shops. He was walking in the middle of the road. The road was likewise new, and street lights loomed.

A car with a boy and a girl in it approached him from behind. They noticed, through the windscreen, a man dressed in traditional attire walking slowly in front of the car.

The boy honked, but the demon remained unmoved. As a result, the boy honked continuously. This infuriated the devil greatly. So, he turned around and made a fist with his hands, saying, "Quebre isso."

All the glass of the car was shattered. Some pieces pricked both the boy and the girl.

"The people of this town are still fools, but now I'm here to teach them some morals." The devil smirked at the car's shadow. He then used his right foot to draw a line in the shadow.

The boy and the girl squealed terribly. They were ripping their clothes and frantically trying to tear their skin. They both exited the car naked and ran here and there. Their skin is turning crimson. The demon was glancing avidly at their blazing shadows.

"I'm the Imperious, and I'm back!" the devil exclaimed, laughing loudly.

They both perished after a period of suffering. Both of their shadows had vanished, and light smoke was emanating from their dead bodies.

Johnny was sound asleep in his home. He received a call informing him that there had been a destructive blast in Poonish's residence, that four corpses had gone missing from the forensic lab, and that two more corpses had been discovered near the market.

He immediately called Ankit, but his phone did not connect. As a result, he quickly left his residence and arrived at the motel. He discovered that Ankit had not been at the motel since the evening. He didn't think it was a coincidence, so he went to the hospital to learn more about the incident.

In the hospital, the doctor examined Poonish and assured Priyanka and Arman that he was fine and would regain consciousness soon.

For both of them, this statement was both comfortable and surprising.

"Doctor, he has suffered a cylinder blast," Ankit explained.

"Are you kidding here, please? It's a hospital," the doctor said as he walked away.

Priyanka and Arman had a lot of questions, and only Poonish could answer them, so they waited in the room for him to regain consciousness.

Johnny eventually arrived at the hospital and headed to Poonish's ward. He was surprised to see Poonish alive and well. Then he approached Priyanka and Arman and inquired as to how all of this had occurred.

Arman gave him the entire incident.

"How about Ankit?" Johnny inquired.

"After the blast, we didn't find him," Arman explained.

Johnny sat in the chair and informed them of the corpses' disappearance.

"What the hell is going on tonight?" Priyanka wondered.

"Something horrible has occurred and is continuing. I believe your friend is involved in all of this," Johnny added.

"What exactly do you want to say?" Arman inquired.

"You understand what I mean. Even a cracker burns people, but that was a cylinder burst," Johnny stated.

"So, you're saying Poonish murdered my sister?" Priyanka asked.

"I'm not sure. We can only speculate; the rest is up to Poonish." Johnny remarked. "I have to leave now, but please contact me as soon as Poonish regains consciousness," and he left.

The Reveal Of Truth

Poonish's condition had not improved despite the passage of 8 hours. The sun came out, but its rays couldn't lift Priyanka and Arman's shroud of worry. They were depressed and fatigued as a result of their lack of sleep. The doctor repeatedly checked Poonish and simply stated that he was fine.

Johnny arrived at the hospital expecting Poonish to have recovered consciousness and told everyone everything, so he brought hot tea for everyone. When he entered the room, however, he found Poonish exactly as he had left him. Priyanka and Arman's mournful expressions destroyed his hopes. Then he gave them tea and began waiting on a chair to relieve their fatigue. Two more hours had been passed.

"I think we're wasting our time here," Johnny said, tired of sitting.

"This is a hospital." "Humanity's last hope," Arman stated.

"Don't be offended, but it's not the last hope," Johnny explained.

Arman and Priyanka were perplexed.

"God! "I think we should go to church," Johnny suggested.

Priyanka and Arman exchanged glances.

"You had both witnessed that incident. It was impossible for anyone. Think deeply," Johnny said.

For a little while, they were deafeningly silent.

"Perhaps Johnny is correct. At least, we should try," Arman added.

Arman and Johnny glanced to Priyanka for approval. Priyanka thought for a moment before agreeing to them.

Priyanka stayed with Poonish as Arman and Johnny left.

Johnny escorted Arman to the town's oldest church. The church was well maintained, which is why it looked so beautiful despite being one of the oldest. There was a big yard with little grass in front of the church. Many people were roaming around there.

They entered via the big gate. The father sat on a bench, wearing a black cassock, and he had white hair and white beard.

"Father," Johnny exclaimed.

"Yes, my child," the father replied as he looked at them.

They approached the father and told him about the situation. After hearing about the incident, the father became quite concerned and instructed them to bring that child (Poonish) here right away.

Johnny and Arman rushed out of the church. While the father went to his chamber, he took a spell book, a bottle of holy water, and some candles, which he placed in front of Jesus. They brought Poonish quickly because the church was only a few kilometres away from the hospital, and Priyanka joined them. When the father noticed that Poonish didn't have a shadow, he stated, "Oh, Jesus!"

"Lay this child down in front of Jesus," urged the father.

They did exactly what the father said. Poonish was made to lie down with his head pointed towards Jesus and his feet pointed towards the gate. The father ignited the candles around Poonish. He then took out the book and began reciting a spell. While reciting, he sprinkled holy water on Poonish's body. Unexpectedly, the sky darkened. Poonish's shadow appeared gradually. When they saw this, everyone was taken aback. The shade darkened progressively, and the candles were out when the full shadow was visible.

Poonish got a jolt, which opened his eyes. He looked around and stood up. Priyanka quickly embraced him.

Imperious, on the other hand, was standing in front of a house. The house was old and decaying, but the garden was exquisite. There were several varieties of flowers in the garden, all of which were fresh. He was emotionally looking at them when suddenly he realised something and fumingly looked in the direction of the church.

Everyone in the church had smiles on their faces, but the father's expression was filled with concern.

"How did I get here?" Poonish inquired.

"Imperious," said the father.

"Now, who is he?" Arman inquired.

"The most potent devil. He once completely demolished this town. He was misanthropic. The founding father of this church, with the help of his four followers and a sorcerer, held him captive in the forest by creating a seal. But now that he's free, I'm concerned," the father told everyone.

"How can he be free if there is a seal in the Perigoso?" Johnny inquired.

"The seal has now been broken; Imperious used this child (pointing to Poonish) to get free," the father said.

"I don't understand why, Poonish." Priyanka inquired.

The father had no response to Priyanka's query.

"Because I went into the woods," Poonish stated.

Everyone was stunned when they heard this.

"But it's impossible to get back alive from the Perigoso," Johnny puzzledly stated.

"I'm surprised because Imperious wouldn't pick just anyone," the father stated as he approached

Poonish. "Son, would you like to shed some light on this?"

Poonish was quiet and avoided looking at them.

"He was Ajar (the one who never gets old)," Priyanka explained.

Johnny and Arman were astonished. Johnny now realised why he didn't know anything about Poonish.

"Devil, Imperious, seal, ajar, what the hell is going?" Arman was irritated.

"Did Poonish murder four of them?" Johnny inquired about the father.

"Not exactly; all five doors had to be opened in order to break the seal. The doors could only be opened if five people who had a special relationship with the Imperious sacrificed. That is why the Imperious implanted a piece of his soul in Poonish's body, as a result of which all of Poonish's relations became his relations," the father recounted, continuing, "of the five relations, the first is blood."

"Sakshi," Priyanka said.

"The second one is love."

"Garima," Arman said.

"The third one is a friend," Priyanka said.

"Ankit, sir!" Johnny stated.

"And the fifth is the one with a pure soul,"

"Atul" Poonish stated.

Arman recalled the incident and stated, "He also chased me."

"But you are not my adversary," Poonish stated.

"That's why, luckily, I'm still alive and Ankit is dead," Arman smirked.

"But you never tried on me," Priyanka said to Poonish.

"Because I genuinely love you," Poonish explained, gazing at Priyanka in the eyes.

"And by the way, Garima had filled the column of love." Arman was upset with Poonish and hit a desk violently. "Why did you go there?" he asked, his voice breaking with grief.

"You are right; I am the root cause of all this," Poonish admitted glumly.

"No, that's not what Arman meant," Priyanka reassured Poonish.

"Father! "What should we do now?" Johnny inquired.

"We're going to fight. If we can catch Imperious once, we'll catch him again." Poonish said.

"It's not as simple as you think," the father explained.

"My childhood was spent in Bengal," Poonish told father. I'm used to it all. He stole all of my happiness, and I want vengeance." His eyes were filled with fury.

"I'm with you," Priyanka told Poonish.

"I just want to kill him," Arman snarled.

"I don't want my daughter to live in fear, so I'm also in," Johnny explained.

The father was happy to hear such brave comments. He thought these were innocent individuals yet they still dared to fight with the devil. Instead of being taken away by courage, the father used his senses and said, "I have to tell other fathers about the Imperious; only then can we make a plan."

"Now you can rest," he said, handing Poonish a bottle of holy water and saying, "Jesus will protect you."

The Good Vs The Bad

The father sent emails to other churches informing them about Imperious. Simultaneously, he sent an invitation to everyone for a key meeting.

The father was in the church library, where numerous books were scattered on tables, some of which were black magic texts and others authored by the first father. He was just interested in finding a way to stop Imperious. It was like an arrow in the dark.

The hours seemed to fly past, but he had nothing in his hands. He walked in front of Jesus to pin his hope when he was tired of searching.

"Now that Imperious is free, we must bring him down. Please, God, point us in the right direction. How can we protect this town and its inhabitants from him? "Please God, help us," the father pleaded.

"If you want to recapture Imperious again," the father heard this sound and turned around. There was Imperious, who was sitting on one of the benches. Then he stood up and approached the father, saying, "You have to get permission from him again." Imperious finished his sentence.

Father was frightened, yet he whistled in the dark.

"There's no need to disturb God, especially for me," Imperious smirked.

Then he looked around. "Everything was changed except Jesus and me," he said.

"Why did you come back?" the father questioned, trying not to terrify her.

"Ask your Xavier (first father)," Imperious stated.

"I'm familiar with your story. There is something nice within you. Just surrender to Jesus, and he will forgive all your mistakes," the father explained.

"I thought I was the notorious one, but see I'm not,". Don't believe in rote things." Imperious laughed. "It's not worthwhile for you."

Imperious noticed the father's shadow approaching his feet. He smirked and crept into the shadows.

"Sombra!" he said, but nothing happened.

"It's not going to happen," the father remarked, picking up one of the surrounding candles and blowing it out.

"O meu senhor, castigue ests impio," he began reciting.

As the smoke from the flame touched Imperious, he stumbled and fell backward.

"You also know some tricks." Imperious stepped up and approached the father again.

This time, the father pulled a bottle of holy water from his pocket and chanted, "O meu senhor, castigue ests impio," before sprinkling it on Imperious. As soon as Imperious was hit by holy water drops, he hit the big gate and fell face down.

Inside the father, a sense of assurance arose. Imperious had been lying about this for quite a while.

A black butterfly suddenly appeared in front of the father. Because all of the doors and windows were closed at the time, the father was astounded. The butterfly erupted in an instant, splattering blood across the father's face and clothes.

Imperious approached the father in a flash.

"Now we are equal," he muttered as he stood in the shadow of his father and began reciting his dark spell.

"Eu invoco a morte

Do subterraneo mais escuro

Para aumentar seu poder e

Para trocar seu corpo com sombra"

Wounds began to appear wherever there were blood splatters on the father's body. The father was in a lot of agony and yelling at the moment, and he wasn't terrified of the Imperious. Fear can't touch someone who is facing death.

"I was wrong; I thought you might change," the father continued firmly, "but once a murderer, always a murderer."

Imperious bowed in gratitude.

"She knew what you could become," the father stated.

Imperious' pride was broken in an instant when he heard this, and his smile faded.

"That's why she left you," the father went on to say.

"Shut up," Imperious snarled.

"If she were with you now," Imperious interrupted Father with a "shut up," but Father was not in the mood to stop.

"You would have used her and then killed her, as you did," the father stated.

Imperious eyes were crimson with anger. His scream smashed all of the glass panes. The father's wounds began to bleed and he rose an inch into the air. The father screamed in agony, but it was drowned out by the Imperious shriek.

As soon as the Imperious scream subsided, the father collapsed to the ground and died. The father's body was covered in blood. Imperious took a moment to glance at the dead body before leaving the church.

The rain began to pour.

Poonish, on the other hand, was in the drawing room of Priyanka's house, looking out the window and remembering all his buddies. He was filled with remorse. The raindrops were coming down from the window glass as if the glass were his heart and the drops were his tears.

Priyanka came, tapped his shoulder, and stood beside him. "It's not your fault", she said, consoling him.

"But I'm the medium," he pointed out.

Priyanka held his hand and said, "Imperious would come out sooner or later. We have all seen his power. We can't change the past, but we can change the future by taking a step in the present," she was encouraging him, just as the doorbell rang.

She was about to go open the door, but Poonish stopped him. He considered that it might be Imperious, so he went and opened the door.

There was Johnny, who was drenched. He entered the house with a tensed expression. Arman also came downstairs.

"What happened?" Arman inquired of Johnny.

Priyanka brought Johnny a towel.

"Turn on the TV and watch out for the news," Johnny said as he took a towel and began wiping himself off.

Meanwhile, Poonish switched on the television. Every news channel broadcast that all of the town's church fathers had died.

The news took everyone by astonishment.

"He was always ahead of us," Arman was tingly.

"What can we do now, without father?" Priyanka was disappointed.

"He is now invincible," Johnny said.

"You all leave this town; it all started with me and will end with me," Poonish sighed.

"Are you crazy? Can't you see the news? "He'll kill you in a second," Priyanka scolded Poonish.

"So, what should we do? Just keep watching this town be destroyed?" Poonish asked, his face flushed.

Everyone's tongue was covering the veil of silence at the time.

Then they took their seats individually. Poonish sat on the steps, Priyanka sat on the couch, Johnny sat in the chair, and Arman wandered around. Everyone was gripped by despair. Only the hands of the clock were moving; everything else had come to a halt.

Outside, the torrential rain had turned into a drizzle.

Poonish had an idea after pondering for an hour. "First father!" he exclaimed happily.

Everyone in the room was staring at him.

"He can help us," he murmured as he rose to his feet.

"Imperious hasn't come off his head yet," Johnny said sarcastically.

"I know he's dead, but if we know about him, we might get something," Poonish said with a smile.

Priyanka and Johnny were intrigued by the notion, but Arman was not since he sulked with Poonish.

"This is our last ray of hope; we have to follow it," Priyanka was convincing Arman.

"What's the plan?" Arman said of Poonish after a little quiet.

"You and Priyanka will go to the central library." Johnny and I will go to church. "The goal will be to gather as much information as possible about the first father," Poonish added.

On the other hand, all of these were conversing, and Imperious was sitting on the pathway in front of that same old house.

"It's been really hard without you. I wish you could be here," he said, his attitude indicating he was missing someone.

The following morning, with the first rays of sunlight, all four set out for their respective destinations. Although the rain had stopped, there was still moisture in the air. The temperature had dropped.

When Priyanka and Arman arrived at the central library, they went straight to the history section. Arman got out the cultural history books and Priyanka started reading the Goa history books.

While Poonish and Johnny, on the other hand, went to the church. Where the funeral was being performed. The hall was packed with people dressed in black. The father's body was placed in the coffin in front of Jesus. Poonish went to the coffin. He felt bad seeing his father's body.

"I'm sorry, father," he said gloomily.

He thought it was his obligation to attend the burial, so he sat with Johnny on one of the benches. People came in one by one, expressing their feelings for the father and saying a few words. When the time came, some people approached the coffin and placed some of Father's belongings inside. The coffin was then carried to the graveyard. Where the father was buried according to all the rituals and where a gravestone was erected. People began to leave slowly, except for Poonish and Johnny, who sat under a tree.

"Being like you're a blessing," Johnny told Poonish.

"Curse, I would like to say," Poonish replied, "I have buried more loved ones than the people you have met so far."

"Don't get me wrong, but don't you think the situation would have been different if you weren't here?" Johnny inquired.

"Maybe or maybe not," Poonish stopped for a moment, sighed coldly, and then continued, "I've always kept myself away from any kind of relationship." I don't know why I couldn't stop myself this time. I miss everyone, especially Sakshi. She was like my little princess."

"I understand your feelings, but we need to focus now," Johnny stated.

"You start, and I'll be there in 5 minutes," Poonish responded.

Johnny stood up and walked away.

Poonish was so engrossed in his memories that he didn't realise five minutes had turned into an hour. When he received a call from Johnny, he emerged from the world of memories, and as he stood up to leave, he noticed a grave with a small hut around it. That grave belonged to Father Xavier. Poonish was in a rush, so he didn't pay attention to it and exited the cemetery.

The Ultimate Clue

Poonish and Johnny returned to Priyanka's house after their quest. Poonish, by the way, used to live in this house after the blast, so it now belonged to him as well. Poonish and Johnny were both unable to obtain much information and were now hoping that Priyanka and Arman would get something.

Despite the passage of time, Arman and Priyanka did not appear. Their phone had also gone out of service. Poonish's head began to fill with anxiety. After a while, he decided to look for them, but as soon as he opened the door, Priyanka and Arman were there in front of him.

Poonish exhaled a sigh of relief and embraced Priyanka as Arman entered and sat on a chair.

"How come it took so long? I was terrified," Poonish said.

"Don't worry, I'll always be in your heart," she said as she kissed his cheeks.

"Did you find anything," Johnny inquired.

"A lot," Arman replied, "and you?"

Johnny yawned and muttered, "Trivial details."

Then they were all set.

Priyanka began narrating.

"The first father named was Xavier Oliveira. He was a Portuguese scholar from a priestly family. He was fascinated by Indian culture; therefore, he travelled to India in 1878 and spread his knowledge from place to place. When the Portuguese were declining from India and they had only Goa and Puducherry, the Portuguese government decided to spread their culture and so they become a part of Indian history. The government decided to build a church in this town to do this. They built the first church in town in 1888. Xavier was the suitable person to be the church's father, and so it was. Xavier was the first to become this town church's father. His brother Artur also came to India in 1990; he was an herbalist. The two brothers made this town flourish, but in early 1906, more than half of the town's population was found dead."

"Some books say it was the plague; others say it was famine," Arman added.

"Maybe it was imperious; remember, father told us about this?" Johnny speculated. "Poonish, do you know about this?" Johnny inquired.

"No, except for the fact that it is my birth year," Poonish said.

"You're very young," Johnny jested.

Everyone simply disregarded him.

"What about the father and his brother in the aftermath of this incident?" Poonish inquired.

"Father survived the incident, but his brother died," Priyanka explained.

"The most surprising thing is that the father hasn't written a book or kept a journal since 1906, while his writings were published every year," Arman puzzledly stated.

Poonish instantly remembered the funeral scene, where some of the father's belongings were kept in the casket with his body. "Maybe he wrote but not published," he informed them of what he witnessed at the funeral.

"So, now we have to go to every cemetery and find the first father's grave," Arman said.

"Don't worry, I found it," Poonish responded.

"Then, what are we waiting for? Let's go," Arman said as he rose up.

"This is not the right time. We have to do this work while avoiding people," Johnny advised.

"Do we have to wait until the evening?" Poonish said.

"It's not a good idea to go to the cemetery at night," Priyanka added.

"I guess we'll have to wait till dawn," Johnny said.

Everyone agreed with this opinion. The day had covered itself with the cloak of the evening, so Johnny left for home. Here, all three had food and started waiting for the morning.

When Johnny arrived at his house, he noticed a swarm of black butterflies hovering over it. He became concerned and ran inside, but the door was locked. He began knocking on the door and shouting his wife's and daughter's names. But there was no response from within. He became so terrified that he was determined to shatter the door, and after three failed attempts, he eventually broke the door and entered the house.

As he went inside, he saw his wife cooking in the kitchen. Seeing Johnny gasping, his wife asked, "What happened to you?"

"I was shouting—why were you not opening the door?" Johnny said. His senses flew away again when his wife told him that she hadn't heard any sound of him at all.

"Where Is Hannah?" he asked in a worried tone.

The sound of shouting suddenly emerged from Hannah's room on the first floor. They both dashed upstairs to the room. Hannah, who was just ten years old, was crying, concealing her face in a corner of the room. They both approached her, hugged her, and attempted to calm her.

When Johnny asked her, Hannah pointed to her tab. Johnny noticed a picture of his house on the tab. Which had become a total shambles, with the same swarm of butterflies hovering over the house. The swarm of butterflies was still present when he peeked through the window. When his wife asked about what happened, the wrinkles on his face revealed his fear.

Poonish and Arman got ready before the sun came up the next day. They brought a large number of digging implements with them. Priyanka had yet to leave her room.

"Come on, Priyanka," Poonish said.

"Johnny hasn't arrived either," Arman said to himself.

"Guys! "Johnny has left the town," Priyanka said as she exited the room.

"What?" Arman and Poonish both spoke up.

"When there is a choice between family and death, everyone chooses family," Priyanka remarked.

"This is our battle. We can't endanger someone else's life," Poonish remarked.

"We should go now," Arman replied, and then they walked to the graveyard.

There was a lot of peace in the crematorium. A sound was coming when the cold wind was hitting the leaves. They secretly entered the crematorium. Poonish brought them to Father Xavier's grave, which was in the centre of the cemetery. They got out their tools, and the boys started digging while Priyanka looked around.

Because the ground was so hard, they had to moisten it in between digs. They became sweaty and short of breath while digging. They'd dig for a while, then fill their lungs for a bit. After digging 5 feet, they discovered the coffin. Both removed the nails from the coffin and opened it. A skeleton wearing a scarf and a locket with a Christian emblem was found in the casket. Many other items were kept in the coffin, but the skeleton's right hand was holding a book.

"We got it." Priyanka picked up the book. Then they buried the grave just as it was and went from there.

The rays of the sun had completely spread by the time they came home. They sat in the living room together to read that book. Because the book was very old, it was damp, and the pages were yellow. Poonish gently opened it and began reading.

"Jan 15, foi um dia lindo e exausto,"

"Portuguese," Arman said.

Priyanka took the book, scanned the page with her phone, translated, and began reading.

"It was a beautiful and exhausting day. Today, we met a lot of traders, peasants, and scholars, but they didn't have enough knowledge about the herbs. So, I decided to stay some more days with Artur in here, Bengal."

She read some more lines.

"It's just a regular diary. What we get after working so hard a diary," Arman grumbled. "This is nonsense," Arman said as he walked up the stairs to his room.

"I too believe the plan is ineffective. We made a mistake," Priyanka murmured glumly as she headed to her room, but Poonish was not convinced. He pondered why his father only kept this diary with him. He translated every page of the diary to find out the solution.

The Imperious, who was watching all this drama standing outside of Priyanka's house. He was about to enter the house suddenly; his eyes fell on the same flowers in the garden that were in the old house. He stopped and smiled, saying, "We'll meet soon," and looked at Poonish through the window. When Poonish felt that someone was staring at him, he looked through the diary. "Strange," Poonish murmured, returning his attention to the diary.

He eventually finished reading the diary but found nothing. He was frustrated, so he threw the diary on the table, which turned it upside down.

He yawned and then stood up. He went into the kitchen, fetched a bottle of cold water from the fridge, first cleaned his face, and then drank the water. He returned to the drawing room feeling a little more revived. His attention returned to the diary. The rear cover of the diary was crumpled and not covered properly. He took the diary and opened the cover. He discovered a folded and concealed page in the back cover. He translated it again because it was in Portuguese.

"If you're reading this, it means the imperious is now free. I knew there would come a time when he would be free, and that was what scared me the most. So, from the moment we captured him, I was looking for a way to kill him. After five years of searching, I discovered that he derives all of his powers from a dark spell. He can be killed if the spell is recited backwards."

Whatever was Witten after that got erased due to dampness. Poonish got on tenterhooks after not getting the next paragraph from the page. So, he called Priyanka.

Arman on the other hand was in a bad mood. So, he decided to work to divert his attention, which is why he got out his office laptop. He became very emotional when he saw a photo of all of them on the display of his laptop. Instead of working, he began looking at images of his friends gloomily.

Among those pictures was Poonish who became an important member of his family. He began to regret placing all of the blame on Poonish.

Going through the pictures, he discovered a video that was the CCTV footage from the day he touched the dead with an inch. He watched Poonish transformed into a fiend and say something in another language. Poonish and Priyanka enter his room. They had the same old piece of paper.

"Look what we discovered." Priyanka handed over her phone to Arman so he could read the translation.

"All we need is just a dark spell," Poonish explained.

"And he'll be finished," Priyanka replied excitedly.

After reading the translation, Arman showed them the video, saying, "Maybe it's the spell."

"Yes! Yes! Yes! It is!" Priyanka exclaimed. Arman's face brightened when he saw Priyanka's excitement, but Poonish's complete attention was on the video, which he was watching repeatedly.

"It's incomplete," Poonish said.

"What?" Priyanka and Arman's joy had come to an end.

"If the spell had been completed, Arman would have died. As it has been happening," Poonish stated.

Priyanka and Arman realised it. Once again, sorrow had arrived at Priyanka's home.

"We always cross the river but drown on the shore," stated Arman.

"Where will we get the remaining part?" Priyanka asked as she sat on the bed.

Various ideas crossed their minds, but none of them were useful.

"I believe it is time to confront him. One of us will go in front of Imperious, and when he recites the spell, the other will quickly reverse it," Poonish explained.

Quietness covered the surroundings. Arman and Priyanka stared at him.

"No! We'll find a book, go to another church, or do anything but not this," Priyanka expressed her disappointment.

She was only looking at Poonish when tears welled up in her eyes, so she left the room to hide them.

"You are right. I'll do it," Arman stated.

"I'll go in front of Imperious, and you'll speak the spell," Poonish remarked as he approached Arman.

"No! "You'll cast the spell," Arman stated.

They were debating because they understood that whoever went in front of the imperious had a worse chance of survival.

"Arman! I started it all, and I'm confident I'll finish everything. I have complete faith in you," Poonish said.

Arman's rage had subsided and he embraced Poonish. After convincing Arman, Poonish went to Priyanka, who was crying on the couch in her bedroom. Priyanka had a hunch that Poonish would be separated from her after this. That's why she was upset.

Poonish sat next to her and began wiping away her tears.

"I'll also come with you," Priyanka sobbed.

"It will be dangerous for you," Poonish said.

"Will there be no danger for you?" Either both or neither go. It's final," Priyanka declared.

Poonish didn't want to endanger her, but he succumbed to Priyanka's obstinacy. So, he just hugged her.

"Nothing can happen to us as long as we are with each other," Poonish stated.

"You forgot about me," Arman remarked from behind, joining Priyanka and Poonish in an embrace.

The Final Chase

It was evening. The whole sky was overcast. It appeared that it would rain. All three were prepared with the plan. According to the diary, Poonish told them that the location where Perigoso was located had previously been wrecked by the devil and that we would find his house in the centre of the forest.

Poonish kept the bottle of holy water provided to him by the father in the back pocket of his cargo pants, while Arman scrawled the half-spell on a piece of paper. Priyanka cleaned the jeep because she hadn't driven it since Garima's death. They all boarded and took off for Perigoso.

They were all dead silent. On one hand, they were terrified, but on the other, they were confident in their plan. They eventually arrived at Perigoso's north-eastern entrance.

Arman gave over the gallery's key to Poonish, saying, "If I couldn't return from the forest, you'd look after the gallery," but Poonish refused and replied, "We'd return together."

After that, they walked into the forest. There were many houses that were now in ruins, and trees peered out from some houses.

"This is terrifying!" Priyanka exclaimed as she looked around.

"How painful it must have been for those who lived here!" Arman added.

"That's why everyone is so scared of him," Poonish explained.

They just kept going. They all came to a halt when they noticed a house with a swarm of butterflies fluttering above it. The residence was slightly better than the rest. Some of the window panes were broken, while others were not. Because of the dampness, the yellow paint had become black in several places. Its roof had also been partially shattered. They realised it was the devil's mansion.

Poonish took a deep breath and looked at both of them to cheer himself up before proceeding to the main gate, which was built of wood. He gave the gate a tiny shove after reaching the door, and it opened. He stepped inside, while Arman and Priyanka hid outside beside the window. The inside view was vastly different from the outside.

A red velvet carpet lay on the ground. There were steps on the front side, a shelf on the left side with numerous old and different wines, and a table with fruits and a knife on the right side. Three chairs were arranged around the table. Electric lamps were mounted on the wall. Everything was pretty old at the place. He seemed to have arrived in the twentieth century.

"Welcome, mate," Imperious said as he walked downstairs.

They were all seeing him for the first time. When he arrived, there was a sense of dread.

"I apologies! I was unable to see you earlier. I was quite busy," he paused for a second, "but thank you; I've been able to be free because of you." Imperious added, walking towards the shelf, "what would you like to drink?"

"I'm not here to drink with you. I've come here to make you repent of your mistakes," Poonish raged.

Imperious smirked, filled a glass with scotch, and came in front of Poonish. He took a sip and said, "So, you finally got something from the diary."

Poonish was astounded to hear this, as were Arman and Priyanka.

"Where's your second, eh! My fault, your first girlfriend. Her sister was madly in love with me. Poor girl. I guess I hurried a bit; I should have enjoyed some more. You know what I mean." Imperious winked and laughed.

Poonish's wrath had reached a boiling point. He tightened his fist and braced himself for a punch, but he couldn't move an inch. What was happening puzzled him. His attention was then pulled to his own shadow, which Imperious was standing in. He shifted his attention back to the ground. He considered it odd that his shadow was visible while the imperious shadow was not.

Priyanka and Arman became enraged as well.

"Just spoke the fucking spell," Arman said.

"I want to see him suffer," Priyanka cursed him.

"How are you going to kill me when you can't even touch me?" Imperious said.

Poonish recognised that he couldn't kill him like this. So, he inhaled twice and exhaled deeply to calm himself, and then he considered how he could have provoked him. That's why he started remembering what was written in the diary.

A smile appeared on Poonish's face. "I won't kill you because you've been dead since you killed Swadheenta," he stated.

The haughty smile of Imperious faded as soon as Swadheenta's name came up.

"Who is this Swadheenta?" Arman asked Priyanka.

"How would I know," Priyanka replied.

"You humans only believe in what is beneficial to you. You don't know either me or her," Imperious remarked solemnly as he finished his glass.

Poonish talked about Swadheenta more after seeing his cause succeed.

"I think, not Garima; Swadheenta was insane, which is why she fell in love with a monster like you.

And I'm sure you must have had a great time with her. "You know what I mean," he winked.

With wrath in his eyes, the demon smashed the glass in his palm.

"Did you...?" Imperious yelled "Cala boca (shut up)" before Poonish could finish his statement. All of the bottles on the shelf had been broken, and all of the liquor had been spilled on the carpet. Imperious became much more dangerous.

"Till now I was very calm because you had a favour on me, but now meet the real Imperious." He stated.

Poonish fulfilled his motive. Now, it was Arman's turn to take this to its ultimate end.

"Eu invoco a morte

Do subterraneo mais escuro

Para aumentar seu poder e

Para trocar seu corpo com sombra"

Imperious recited the spell.

Arman and Priyanka were paying close attention to the spell.

All of the butterflies that had been hovering over the house suddenly descended and began circling around Poonish. They appeared to be forming a storm around him. Poonish was lifted a foot in the air by the storm. All of the broken glass that was on the ground joined the storm. The fragments got more lethal as the storm accelerated and began tearing Poonish's skin from every angle.

Poonish was screaming terribly in pain while Imperious took pleasure in seeing him.

Arman quickly wrote the full spell and said, "Now, it's your turn, fucking devil," and started reciting the spell backwardly.

"Sombra com corpo seu trocar para

E poder seu aumentar para

Escuro mais subterraneo do"

Imperious heard a faint sound of recitation of a spell. He looked everywhere but couldn't find it. He noticed a few Arman hairs when he looked out the window to his left. Arman had come too close to the window to hear the spell. Imperious instantly moved his hand to the window.

"Quebre isso!" he shouted.

Arman was drawn inside by an invisible force; that's why he fell on the carpet, breaking the glass, but the paper on which the spell was written slipped from his grasp and dropped outside. Priyanka, who was standing there, quickly ran behind the house. Arman's body was covered in glass shards, with one enormous shard embedded in his neck.

In the midst of all this, the storm that had been swirling around Poonish vanished, as did the butterflies. Poonish had also fallen to the ground, and his condition had worsened to the point that he couldn't stand and his skin was tattered.

Imperious came to Arman and said, "Eventually you got to know. This means you are also going to meet everyone else now."

Arman attempted to utter the final phrase of the spell to kill him, but only blood gushed out of his mouth. Meanwhile, Priyanka took that paper and hid beside the main gate. She started reciting the spell in a very low voice.

"Say bye to your friend." Imperious remarked, and he was going to use his feet to press the glass embedded in Arman's neck when Poonish mustered his remaining strength and lunged towards Imperious, to grab him, but his effort was futile as Imperious flung him aside with his left hand. Poonish fell over the table, breaking it as well as the bottle of holy water he had in his back pocket. The holy water spilled on the carpet, and the knife and the fruits fell into the water.

Even before Priyanka accomplished the last phrase of the spell, Imperious pressed the piece of glass that slit Arman's throat, and he died in agony for a second.

When the spell was finished, Imperious let out a loud yell and collapsed, clutching his head.

Priyanka hurried to Arman's body and sobbed. Poonish was also crying as he moved towards Arman's body.

The memories that surface after someone passes away are usually traumatic. It hurts a lot not to see the individual again in life.

Their faces were wet with tears. Poonish held himself responsible for Arman's death. They were mourning the loss when suddenly Priyanka shrieked, grasping her hair.

They couldn't figure out what was happening until Poonish turned around and spotted Imperious standing in Priyanka's shadow.

"Ir para cima", Imperious said, stepping out from Priyanka's shadow. Priyanka's shadow, which was on the ground, moved to the front wall in a jiffy. Slowly, the shadow started rising upward, due to which Priyanka also started rising upward in the air.

Someone seemed to be clutching Priyanka's hair and tugging her upwards. She was crying and yelling.

Poonish crawled forward to save her, but Imperious kicked him off, causing him to fall near the broken table.

You're very curious about Swadheenta. Feel the anguish of separation now, and then you get your all answers."

The longer Priyanka hung; the more pressure built up on her head. As a result, blood began to flow from the hair roots. She was yearning a lot.

Poonish was helpless as he watched his love in distress. He lowered his face, thinking they were defeated. He thought that they recited the spell upside down, but nothing happened. He thought it was the last time.

He had, however, forgotten that God was with him. After a gust of wind touched his face, Poonish regained consciousness. Suddenly, he noticed the imperious shadow near his feet.

"Shadow," he mumbled, and he remembered his aunt's words that devils always hide their bodies.

"Alas! I spilled all my wine. The slowly dying always makes me feel alive", Imperious said and began staring at Priyanka.

Poonish instantly grabbed up the knife in front of him and sliced his hand, so that his blood could be added to the knife along with holy water, and stabbed it directly into the shadow of Imperious.

Priyanka tripped and fell on the carpet. Imperious turned to face Poonish and began yelling angrily. Holy water came out of his heart, and after that, flames engulfed his shadow.

"I'll come back" The final words of Imperious to Poonish before he was consumed by fire.

Priyanka, whose face was smeared in blood, staggered to Poonish, hugged him, and cried profusely. Poonish later knew that the spell didn't kill Imperious but only showed his shadow. There were ashes on one side and Arman's body on the other. They lost everything, even after winning.

Two days later, Priyanka and Poonish cremate Arman along with Sakshi, Garima, Atul and Sahil, according to the rituals.

They had painful memories attached to this town, so they decided to go to Indore.

After a month, Poonish and Priyanka relocated to Indore, Madhya Pradesh. They started Arman's gallery there, and afterwards they got married.

A year later, they were blessed with a baby boy.

In the hospital, all the babies were in the babies' ward. Poonish's kid was also there. Everyone was asleep, and all the children were covered in blankets.

Suddenly Poonish's boy's blanket slowly slides down, and he smiled. Surprisingly, his tiny teeth showed up on the day he was born. Then he opened his eyes, one of which was normal but the other was crimson like Imperious.

TO BE CONTINUED……… in Part 2.

About the Author

Nitin Sharma was born in Mathura, Uttar Pradesh. But the age of 1, his family moved to Delhi. He is a student and a learner. His father works in a private sector and his mother is a homemaker. He has a lifelong fascination with storytelling. At the age of 10, he began reading Panchatantra. When he read Aruthur Conan Doyle's 'The Hound of the Baskervilles' in class 12th, he realized what he wanted to do with his life and he choose to became a writer.

Following his 12th, he wrote a 10 page short tale titled Imperious in 2015. After that, he read more books and learnt how to write. His short story evolved into a novel in 2023. Between these years, he wrote rough draft of the 2nd part of Imperious as well as two other stories. The first novel of his Universe is Imperious.

www.ingramcontent.com/pod-product-compliance
Lightning Source LLC
LaVergne TN
LVHW041851070526
838199LV00045BB/1538